# He'd Tracked Her Down.

Her memories hadn't done this cowboy justice. She'd forgotten how handsome he was. Six feet of solid muscle. And oh what he could do with those muscles.

"Caleb."

A passion so hot she nearly ignited replaced the surprise in his eyes, and then he scowled. "What in the hell are you doing here?"

"I live here. I bought the ranch."

"*You* bought the ranch?" His voice was filled with anger and disbelief.

"Yes," Brooke replied, "for my motivational retreat."

His broad shoulders relaxed. "Good. Then you won't need the pastures."

"Why are you concerned about my land?" she asked.

"I live next door. For the last ten years I've leased acreage from the previous owner for my herd. I need to continue."

*He lived next door*. All she had to do to be reminded of the night she'd lost control and loved every minute of it was look over the fence. She struggled for calm and reason. "Caleb, I think you'd better come inside...."

Dear Reader,

Let Silhouette Desire rejuvenate your romantic spirit in May with six new passionate, powerful and provocative love stories.

Our compelling yearlong twelve-book series DYNASTIES: THE BARONES continues with *Where There's Smoke...* (#1507) by Barbara McCauley, in which a fireman as courageous as he is gorgeous saves the life and wins the heart of a Barone heiress. Next, a domineering cowboy clashes with a mysterious woman hiding on his ranch, in *The Gentrys: Cinco* (#1508), the launch title of THE GENTRYS, a new three-book miniseries by Linda Conrad.

A night of passion brings new love to a rancher who lost his family and his leg in a tragic accident in *Cherokee Baby* (#1509) by reader favorite Sheri WhiteFeather. *Sleeping with Beauty* (#1510) by Laura Wright features a sheltered princess who slips past the defenses of a love-shy U.S. Marshal. A dynamic Texan inspires a sperm-bank-bound thirtysomething stranger to try conceiving the old-fashioned way in *The Cowboy's Baby Bargain* (#1511) by Emilie Rose, the latest title in Desire's BABY BANK theme promotion. And in *Her Convenient Millionaire* (#1512) by Gail Dayton, a pretend marriage between a Palm Beach socialite and her millionaire beau turns into real passion.

Why miss even one of these brand-new, red-hot love stories? Get all six and share in the excitement from Silhouette Desire this month.

Enjoy!

Melissa Jeglinski
Senior Editor, Silhouette Desire

# The Cowboy's Baby Bargain

## EMILIE ROSE

Published by Silhouette Books
**America's Publisher of Contemporary Romance**

Thanks, Dad,
for always being there for me and my boys. And thanks to Heart of Carolina Romance Writers, my support team.

SILHOUETTE BOOKS

ISBN 0-373-76511-8

THE COWBOY'S BABY BARGAIN



This edition published by arrangement with Harlequin Books S.A.



Visit Silhouette at www.eHarlequin.com

**Printed in U.S.A.**

**Books by Emilie Rose**

Silhouette Desire

*Expecting Brand's Baby* #1463
*The Cowboy's Baby Bargain* #1511

---

## *EMILIE ROSE*

lives in North Carolina with her college sweetheart husband and four sons. This bestselling author's love for romance novels developed when she was twelve years old and her mother hid the books under sofa cushions each time Emilie entered the room. Emilie grew up riding and showing horses. She's a devoted baseball mom during the season and can usually be found in the bleachers watching one of her sons play. Her hobbies include quilting, cooking (especially cheesecake) and anything cowboy. Her favorite TV shows include the Discovery Channel's medical programs, *ER, CSI* and *Boston Public.* Emilie's a country music fan because there's an entire book in nearly every song.

Emilie loves to hear from her readers and can
be reached at P.O. Box 20145, Raleigh, NC 27619
or at http://www.EmilieRose.com.

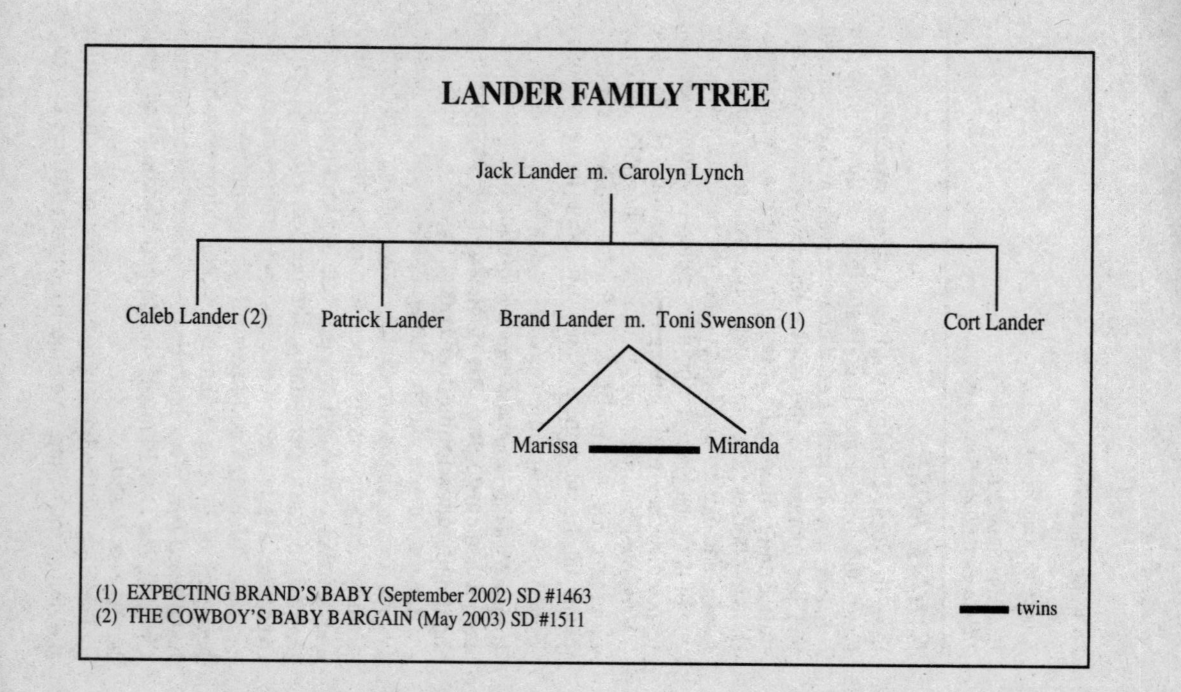
LANDER FAMILY TREE
Jack Lander m. Carolyn Lynch
Caleb Lander (2)
Patrick Lander
Brand Lander m. Toni Swenson (1)
Cort Lander
Marissa
Miranda
(1) EXPECTING BRAND'S BABY (September 2002) SD #1463
(2) THE COWBOY'S BABY BARGAIN (May 2003) SD #1511
twins

# One

Brooke Blake picked up her beer, sipped and grimaced. Success was an acquired taste. Evidently, so was the bitter, yeasty brew in the longneck bottle. But she was determined to experience *everything* her new home state had to offer—including the beer bottled here.

Glancing at her watch, she granted herself ten minutes to brood over the contradictory state of her life. Professionally, her success as a bestselling motivational author and speaker continued to rise, but her credibility was in jeopardy because personally, she needed a lifestyle makeover. She'd failed to achieve her most important goal *ever.*

She'd calculated and taken all the appropriate steps, but her goal of having a family by her thirty-fifth birthday had eluded her. What had she overlooked in her approach? Opening her Day Planner, she flipped back until she found her five-year plan.

The door of the bar opened. A draft of fresh air stirred the smoke hovering over the room and ruffled the pages of her planner. Lifting her gaze to the mirror behind the bar, she studied the cowboy's reflection when he paused to survey the room. Until the door closed behind him the fading afternoon light silhouetted his slim hips and broad shoulders. Nice, but alas, not her type. The only Remingtons she wanted to possess were cast in bronze and made to sit on a mantel. This guy looked like he could have posed for the artist. All he needed were chaps, a horse and a lariat thrown over his shoulder.

He crossed the hardwood floor with the grace of an athlete and the presence of a man used to leading not following. She was abundantly familiar with the type and had discovered that most of them felt threatened by a successful woman.

Specifically her.

He made his way toward the bar and stopped behind her, catching her gaze in the mirror. She hoped he hadn't considered her scrutiny an invitation, but was prepared to correct him if he had. Unwanted attention was a part of her job. She turned to face him and forgot all about the polite rejection she'd mastered years ago.

The cowboy's reflection in the cloudy mirror hadn't done him justice. The hard angles and planes of his face were too rough to be classified as handsome, but she found him compelling regardless. Dark stubble covered a stubborn, square jaw with an incredibly sexy cleft. In his long-sleeved chambray shirt, opened just enough to reveal dark chest hair, and Wranglers snug enough to reveal rather impressive territory, he could have stepped right off the pages of a calendar geared toward women with Wild West fantasies.

Specifically, not her. She preferred the academic type.

His gaze drifted over her the way the lazy stream wandered over her new ranch—slow and easy with numerous detours. His eyes, the rich brown of coffee beans, affected her like a shot of espresso. Unwelcome awareness rippled through her, settling in the pit of her stomach.

He removed his hat, revealing thick, glossy hair the same coffee-rich shade. ''Mind if I sit?''

His voice was middle-of-the-night-secrets deep, and his soft, full lips were made to whisper sweet nothings in some woman's ear. But not hers. She liked her men more refined, more...urban, but for a moment she wondered what it would be like to make love to a man as primitive as this one. She seriously doubted it would be the kind of silent, civilized coupling to which she'd become accustomed. This man would be earthier, noisier. More adventurous.

Shutting down her improper, but stimulating, mental meanderings, she straightened her shoulders and glanced around the room. She'd been so intent on discovering the glitch in her goals that she hadn't noticed the bar filling. The only empty seat was the one beside hers.

Her type or not, the cowboy would be sharing her space. She lifted her purse from the stool beside her and hung it on the wooden slatted back of her own. ''Be my guest.''

''Thanks.'' As he settled his long, lean frame onto the stool his knee brushed her thigh. She wondered if he'd done it on purpose, but he didn't try to extend the contact. '''Scuse me, ma'am.''

Instead of rubbing the tingling spot where they'd touched, she clenched her hand around the amber bottle in front of her and lifted it to moisten her suddenly dry mouth. She shuddered as the now tepid beverage filled her mouth and then forced herself to swallow. She'd never acquire a taste for this stuff.

Cowboys, on the other hand, were a different story. If the ones she would encounter once she moved into her new home looked and smelled as good as this one she probably wouldn't have any trouble finding the right man to settle down with her on her ranch. However, she would prefer one a little less rough around the edges. A cultured cowboy—if there were such a thing.

She picked up her pen and wrote in her planner. *Failure is a temporary condition.* She felt slightly better so she added another line. *Any goal is attainable if approached in the proper manner.* So where had she veered off the path to her goal of finding a husband?

The men in her life thus far had either resented the time she devoted to her career or wanted to ride on the coattails of her success. She drew a vertical line on the page and listed their names in one of two categories: *Users* or *Losers.*

In her peripheral vision she saw the cowboy settle his hat on his opposite knee and lift a finger to signal for the bartender. She could feel his assessing gaze on her. "I would have taken you for a chardonnay drinker."

She shrugged without looking his way and forced down another noxious sip of beer. It grew more disgusting by the moment. "You'd have been right, but when in Rome..."

The bartender approached. "What can I get you?"

"Tequila. Straight. Better make it a double shot. You have any white wine back there for the lady?"

"Sure. Coming right up."

She didn't want him to get the idea that she was here to pick up a man. That would have to wait until she'd moved into her new home, and then she'd be looking for Mr. Right, not Mr. July. A vision of the cowboy wearing nothing but a staple in his navel flashed in her mind. The image practically jolted her out of her seat. Nudie magazines had never been a favorite of hers, and yet here she was with visions of cowboy buns dancing in her head.

She turned quickly and their legs bumped again—this time her fault. "Pardon me. You don't have to buy me a drink."

"I do if I don't want to watch you making that face. Looked like you were choking down cough medicine."

She hadn't blushed in years, but to her surprise heat climbed her cheeks. She tucked her chin and ran a fingernail beneath the edge of the bottle's label. ''I've never been crazy about beer.''

''No kidding.'' She heard laughter in his voice. Out of the corner of her eye she studied his big, tanned hands. Numerous scars crisscrossed the backs, but his nails were clean and neatly trimmed. He shelled a peanut from the bowl on the bar one-handed and popped it into his mouth. ''So what are you crazy about—besides making lists?''

Brooke closed her planner. She absolutely refused to discuss her failures, and it was no one's business that she'd have to start on her goal of having a family alone. She wasn't about to confess to some stranger that tomorrow she had an appointment to be artificially inseminated.

The uneasy feeling in her stomach intensified. Her hands started to shake. She'd thought it out, plotted the pros and cons, and chosen the most appropriate donor. He was blond like her and came from a similar academic background. He'd been carefully screened, had no known medical problems, and was the genetically ideal choice.

Pasting on a sympathetic smile, she faced the cowboy and turned the conversation in a different direction. ''I'm crazy about my work, but let's not talk about me. You ordered a double. It sounds as if you've had a rough day.'' She was a master at pulling information from others and at making even the most pessimistic see the brighter side.

''Worse than some. Better than others.'' He pulled out his wallet and laid a bill on the bar. ''Nobody died.''

A smile twitched her lips at his dry humor. ''That's always positive. Any permanent damage?''

''Prob'ly not.''

The bartender slid their drinks onto the counter. Brooke reached for her purse.

The cowboy shook his head. ''It's on me.''

''Well…thank you, but I really don't think—''

''No buts. Just a drink. I'm not looking for more.''

Taken aback by his frankness, she blinked at him. ''Neither was I.''

"Then you shouldn't come in here dressed like that."

"What's wrong with my suit?" The lavender silk had cost the earth and she dearly loved it. The short skirt showed her legs, and the loosely belted jacket accentuated her waist. She'd bought it when her first book hit the *New York Times* bestseller list. It was her lucky suit. She saved it for her most important occasions. Today qualified. She'd closed on a quaint little ranch fifty miles south of Tilden, Texas.

The rolling hills and sprawling house were almost exactly what she pictured when she closed her eyes and visualized her dream home, but the property would be so much more than just her home. It was perfect for both business and personal reasons. She'd turn the former dude ranch into a corporate retreat, a place to do her life's work without the incessant traveling. It might be a little rustic for her needs right now, but with a little paint, elbow grease and a bulldozer or two, she'd whip the property into shape.

He sipped his drink and winced at the bite of raw liquor. "Besides looking good enough to eat, you're dressed like money. This bar is close enough to the courthouse that some of the delinquents drop in. Better keep your purse in your lap."

Flustered by his backhanded compliment, she glanced around the room again, this time noting the less than professional—all right, *seedy*—appearance of the other clientele and pulled her purse into her lap. She hadn't noticed earlier because she'd been rushing to find a seat and examine her new deed. For the first time in her life she owned land. She patted her bag. Just knowing the deed was inside filled her with a sense of accomplishment. One goal out of three wasn't a total washout.

"One of the clerks recommended the barbecue here."

He pointed to the low sanitation rating on the wall. She decided to skip the food and pretend she hadn't noticed he didn't wear a ring on his left hand. It wasn't important because she wasn't interested in him that way.

"And you might not want to check out every man who walks in the door the way you did me."

Embarrassment flamed her face. She set her wineglass down with a thump that would have broken more fragile stemware. "I did no such thing."

He eyed her over the rim of his glass. "What color are my boots?"

"Brown—" Another wave of heat scorched her. "Oh, for goodness' sake. Ninety-nine percent of the men here are wearing brown boots."

He pointed his finger like a toy gun and pulled the imaginary trigger. His grin displayed almost-perfect white teeth and a twinkle lit his dark eyes. "Gotcha."

She bit her lip to keep from smiling back. "That wasn't nice."

"At least you've quit scowling over that book like somebody shot your dog. Not kidding 'bout the bar, though. Watch your stuff and don't leave alone. Let me know when you're ready to go. I'll walk you out."

Why would a stranger do such a thing? Whatever the reason, she'd take the gallant cowboy up on his offer. "Thank you. I wouldn't want to spend my birthday at the police station filling out a report."

"Birthday?"

"Yes, I've tacked another year of wisdom and experience onto my belt."

One dark brow rose and a crooked half smile tilted his lips. "You really believe that cr—baloney?"

Brooke cringed as she sipped the acidic wine. "Affirmation is essential to good health and prosperity."

He looked skeptical. "Believing will make it so, huh?"

"Of course. You'll only get out of life what you truly believe you deserve."

He sipped his drink. "You sound like a self-help book."

She should since she was quoting chapter thirteen of her first book. Brooke snapped her teeth shut. It was terribly difficult to keep herself from trying to convert this nonbeliever. "You don't believe in self-prophecy?"

"If folks got what they deserved the world would be a whole different place. Probably a better one. I take it the wine's no better than the beer?"

Obviously she hadn't managed to conceal her shudder as well as she'd thought. "It's not one of California's finest."

"Sweetheart, I hate to tell you, but you're a long way from California."

Before she could respond a fight broke out in the back corner. Just like a bad B movie, one man broke a chair over another's head. Others jumped up to join in.

Her cowboy muttered a curse. "The place around the corner will suit you better."

"I hardly think—" She broke off when a beer bottle came sailing through the air toward her head. In an instant the cowboy had snaked an arm around her waist and yanked her off her chair and practically into his lap. She found her face plastered against a warm chest with the cowboy's rough palm protecting her face. Her hand was…well, somewhere it shouldn't be. She snatched it back, but her skin tingled from the unexpected intimacy.

The sound of breaking glass and the bartender's blistering language splintered the air. Brooke peered between the cowboy's fingers and realized in disbelief that she was in the middle of a barroom brawl—a first for her.

She'd barely had time to register the sound of a steady heartbeat beneath her ear when her cowboy stood, putting himself between her and the chaos. He scooped up her Day Planner and purse from where they'd landed on the floor and shoved both in her hands. "Let's go."

The noise level had risen dramatically, but if she wasn't mistaken, he was ordering her to leave. "Excuse me?"

He shoved his hat on his head, scowled at her, and

leaned forward to growl in her ear, "You're not going to be stupid about this are you?"

She had an IQ in the genius range and opened her mouth to tell him so. A chair flew through the air and crashed less than a yard away. One of the legs broke off and skidded her way, but the cowboy's booted foot stopped it before it hit her. She forgot what she was going to say.

"Let's go," he repeated, grabbing her by the elbow and dragging her toward the door even though neither of them had finished their drinks. Since he had no trouble cutting a path through the exodus of other patrons, she followed in his wake until they'd reached the sidewalk and cleared the entrance. He stopped beneath a streetlight. It blinked on as if sensing their presence in the dusk.

"Where're you parked?"

Looping her purse strap over her shoulder, she wondered why she didn't tell him to take a hike. "By the courthouse, but—"

"Did you want dinner before you hit the road? If you do, I'll walk you to the restaurant around the corner and buy you another drink before I go." It wasn't the most gracious invitation she'd ever heard.

She was an independent woman. She shouldn't find his behavior gallant or attractive, but she did. None of the men in her life had ever made her feel so…protected. It was a peculiar feeling, one she wanted to explore.

"Why don't you join me for dinner instead?"

He blinked. His lashes were as lush and sexy as the rest of him. "What makes you so sure I'm not one of the courthouse delinquents?"

She was very good at reading people. Her cowboy's gaze was direct and his body posture said he had nothing to hide. "You have an honest face."

He laughed. It was a deep rumbling sound that reached down inside her and stirred things up. "Haven't you ever heard that you can't judge a book by its cover?"

Studying people was her vocation. Written somewhere in her notes for her next book were the words: *No one ever enters your life at the wrong time.* Her job was to discover why him and why now. She had to find out what it was about this primitive man that pulled a response from her. "I'm willing to risk it if you are. Can you recommend a place with good Texas-style barbecue?"

His eyes narrowed. "I've never let a woman buy my dinner."

Pride she understood. The men of her acquaintance seemed to have an abundance of it. "I owe you. That bottle would have hit me, and the chair came awfully close. Consider it an opportunity to experience another dimension."

"You're talking like a self-help book again."

She wouldn't tell him why. "I tend to do that."

"It's only dinner you're buying. Understand?" Even in the fading light she could see the dull flush climbing his neck.

The thrill shooting through her at his implication shocked her. What would it be like to buy a man's attentions? She tamped down the inappropriate thought because she wasn't that type of woman. *No,* her conscience prodded, *you're the kind who buys a stranger's sperm and has it sterilely inserted by a doctor at a fertility clinic.*

She wasn't making a mistake, was she? Of course not, she'd considered every angle. Not only was she emotionally and physically ready to become a mother, she had very little time to accomplish the feat. Her own mother had been in full-blown menopause by the time she'd turned forty, topped off by a complete hysterectomy at forty-five. If she wanted a baby her intuition warned her it was now or never. She couldn't waste any more time waiting for Mr. Right to father her child.

That funny feeling started in her stomach again. She tried to ignore it because it was too late for doubts, too late to cancel tomorrow's appointment—even if she wanted to, which she didn't. She considered digging an antacid from her purse. She'd eaten a bottleful since deciding to go through with the insemination, but that was okay. The baby would benefit from both the antacids and the prenatal vitamins she'd started last month after paying the deposit on the vial of sperm.

"Please, join me for dinner. I—I'm sick of my own company." It was a painful admission. She'd always believed you had to be content with yourself before you could be content with anyone else, but tonight she didn't want to be alone with her own thoughts. Her doubts. Her fears.

He ran a hand over his jaw. Immediately she recalled the raspy texture of his palm against her own cheek and wondered what it would feel like scraping against her belly, her breasts. The uneasy feeling in her stomach turned into something else all together. Warmth prickled from her thighs to her breasts.

"I promise not to attack you over the appetizers." She hoped he didn't notice the tremor in her voice.

"Yeah, sure. Why not?" His reluctance wasn't flattering. "Best place for barbecue is about two miles north of town. We'll have to drive. I'm parked near the courthouse, too. You can ride with me or follow."

Despite her foolhardy decision to have dinner with a total stranger, she wasn't stupid enough to get into a car with one. Besides, the restaurant was in the same direction as her motel. "I'll follow you."

He offered a large, tanned hand. "Name's Caleb."

She was so used to being recognized from her public appearances that it never occurred to her that she'd have to introduce herself—not even here in the middle of nowhere, Texas. "Brooke."

No recognition flared in his eyes, but then she doubted cowboys read many goal-actualization books. His hand swallowed hers. During the brief formality her senses registered a multitude of things: strength, heat, rough calluses and *gentleness.* He handled her like she might be breakable instead of trying to prove his masculinity by crushing her hand the way some men did.

Her pulse kicked up a notch. Her breathing became shallow. A smile tugged her lips at the irony of being physically attracted to a man so wrong for her. Fate, it seemed, had a wicked sense of humor.

Maybe she'd fantasize about Caleb tomorrow while the doctor did his thing.

Caleb released her and turned toward their cars. She lengthened her stride and she could tell he shortened his. Pent-up energy marked his every step.

The man truly was a work of art. She was admiring the shadows cast beneath his cheekbones by the streetlights when he turned unexpectedly and caught her staring. "You in town for long?"

"No. Just passing through. Tomorrow I fly to... Dallas." Her stomach tightened again. She told herself it was anticipation not nervousness or doubt. "And you?"

"I had business in town, but the deal fell through." He stiffened his shoulders and looked away.

"I'm sorry. Perhaps you could reexamine the situation and approach again from a different angle?"

He cast her a sideways glance. She glimpsed his crooked smile before he faced forward again. "I'm talking like a self-help book again?"

"Yep."

They came to a corner. He flung his arm in front of her when a car unexpectedly zipped out of a parallel parking space and sped past. The protective gesture sent a warmth through her and not just because his palm briefly touched her belly. Heat transferred through silk like nobody's business.

"You're a regular white knight, aren't you?"

A flush climbed from his collar. "No, ma'am. You offered to buy my dinner. Not gonna let you renege on it by getting mowed down.''

She didn't believe his blustering for a minute. ''You're full of hooey, Caleb.''

He thumbed the brim of his hat and winked. ''And don't you forget it.''

Brooke laughed. The sound surprised her. She'd been so driven and focused on building her career over the last few years she couldn't remember the last time she'd laughed. The realization sobered her.

''Hey, none of that. You start looking like your dog died again and it'll put me off my food. I'd hate not to enjoy a free meal.''

They reached the parking lot and her rented Miata. It had been a spur-of-the-moment decision—the likes of which she never gave into—to rent the tiny, red sports car. Running a hand over the black convertible top, she realized she hadn't let herself examine the sudden need to be wild and free. It must have something to do with the commitment she'd made. If the insemination succeeded her solo days would be over, and she'd be buying a minivan.

She needed an antacid.

''Second thoughts?''

His deep voice jerked her out of her contemplation. ''Of course not. I've thought it all out. I know exactly what I'm doing.''

His brows rose and she cringed in embarrassment. He'd meant dinner, not her decision to become pregnant by an anonymous donor with a perfect set of vital statistics. She scrambled to cover her faux pas. ''I really do want to try Texas barbecue.''

Caleb looked skeptical, but didn't argue. ''Then follow me. If your taste buds will fit in that toy car, bring 'em along.''

His long athletic stride carried him toward a big, silver pickup. Brooke caught herself ogling his behind and yanked herself back in line. What was wrong with her tonight? It must be that she was nearing ovulation. It couldn't be that she was considering getting wild and crazy with the cowboy.

Was she? Of course not. She'd never do something so foolhardy, so spontaneous. She wasn't the type to take unnecessary risks—even if it would distract her from the clinical procedure she'd undergo tomorrow afternoon.

She opened her purse and dug out an antacid.

# Two

Caleb checked the rearview mirror one more time. The little red car still tailed him.

How long would it take for Brooke—if that was her real name—to come to her senses. Ladies like her didn't waste time on men like him. She was way out of his league. Everything about her—her walk, her talk, her clothes—reeked of culture, class and education. He, on the other hand had none of the above. His ex had made sure he knew it, and he doubted he'd acquired any in the decade since Amanda had left.

He wasn't one to pick up a woman in a bar, but it sure beat the hell out of his original plan of drinking himself into oblivion.

He'd stopped by the courthouse this afternoon hoping whomever had outbid him on the other half of Crooked Creek ranch wouldn't show up with the cash by the five o'clock deadline. As second highest bidder he'd then buy the property by default, and his debt to his family would finally be repaid. The clerk had told him he'd missed the new owner by minutes. The deed had been signed, sealed and delivered, killing his chance to regain his family's land.

He'd already waited ten years. How in the hell long would it take to get this monkey off his back?

He hit his blinker, indicating the restaurant, and pulled into the well-lit gravel lot. The timber building didn't look like much, but they served the best barbecue in all of McMullen County, Texas, behind those faded gray doors. He ate here whenever he had business in the county seat.

Climbing out of his truck, Caleb shoved his keys into his pocket when common sense told him he should've been starting the hour's drive home. Brooke parked beside him. He circled her tiny car and opened her door. When she swung her legs out his mouth went dry. She wasn't wearing stockings. He had to tamp down the urge to stroke her from ankle to thigh to see if her skin felt as silky as it looked. He settled for taking her hand and pulling her from the low seat. Her grip was strong, but her palms were soft. The sight of her deep pink nails wrapped around his fingers set off internal alarm bells.

His ex-wife had been big on manicures, although she'd preferred fire-engine red on her talons. She used to do some pretty amazing things to him with her nails. 'Course, that had been before she'd discovered he wasn't made of clay and that she couldn't bend him into the man she'd wanted him to become. When she discovered he had a backbone, she'd packed up and left. Her leaving had caused one heck of a lot of problems back home—problems he'd continue wrestling evidently since somebody else still held the deed to his land.

Brooke smiled up at him, reminding him that her legs weren't her only asset. She was long and lean, but curved in all the right places. Her eyes were as green as the stock pond on a hot summer day and just as deep. A man could fall in and not want to come out. Short blond hair cupped her chin and framed a face pretty enough to be on the cover of a magazine. Her skin was smooth and pale, as if she didn't spend much time outdoors—another sign they had nothing in common.

It was probably the moonlight making her so beautiful—combined with the fact that he hadn't had sex in longer than he could remember. He'd learned the hard way not to get involved with locals, and he rarely had the time or money to stray far from Crooked Creek.

He let go of Brooke's hand and ran a finger under his collar when what he really needed to do was adjust his undershorts. His mind was taking detours and his body seemed happy to follow. Another minute of that trip and his jeans would cut off circulation to some vital parts.

"What a quaint place." A soft smile curved Brooke's lips.

He wondered if she was insulting the weathered building, but that didn't sound like sarcasm coming from her lips. His mind shifted to far better ways of passing the time with a beautiful woman, ways that didn't involve the width of a table or even a sliver of silk between them. Reining in his stampeding hormones took more effort than it should have.

She'd invited him to dinner. End of story. It was her birthday and she was lonely. He'd decided to accept her invitation because it meant delaying the inevitable of having to look his father and brother in the eye and tell them he'd failed them again. If he'd seen the flare of something more in Brooke's eyes a time or two it didn't mean he'd act on it. For crying out loud, he was thirty-eight not eighteen.

Tell that to his shorts.

She tipped her head back, studied the starry sky and inhaled deeply. "What a beautiful night."

"Yep." He turned toward the restaurant and tried to deny the desire to taste her soft mouth and feel her slender body beneath his. Having the width of the table between them looked better all the time. As long as he didn't touch her again he'd be able to corral his urges. He hoped the smell of southern cooking would soon replace the smell of sweet woman in his nostrils.

An exiting couple opened the restaurant door before he and Brooke reached the porch. A blast of music hit him, and Caleb stopped so fast Brooke ran into him. For a split second her soft breasts pressed just below his shoulder blades and her hips nudged his butt. Electricity jolted through each of his cells as if he'd been hit with a cattle prod.

She frowned. "Pardon me. Is something wrong?"

He'd forgotten the restaurant had live bands on Thursday and Friday nights. The lights would be dimmed, and there'd be candles on the tables. The romantic atmosphere was the last thing he needed. Unlocking his jaw, he struggled to pull himself out of this whirlwind of need. "Band's playing tonight. It'll be loud. Maybe we'd better try someplace else."

Excitement sparkled in her eyes. Damn. Next thing you know, she'd want to dance. "The band sounds wonderful."

The hostess came forward and waved them in. Before he could convince Brooke to leave she'd requested a table for two, and the waitress had led them to a tiny square beside the dance floor.

Caleb's stomach sank. The woman was already overloading his circuits and his common sense. Close body contact would fry his brain for sure. What he ought to do was go back to the seedy bar and get knee-walking drunk. He could sleep it off in his truck and go home tomorrow as planned.

He sure as hell didn't need to spend an evening with a woman who had a five-year plan. He'd read that much in Brooke's notebook before she'd closed it. His ex had made lists, too. He'd do best to remember that women—

including the one tapping her toes across the table from him—always had an agenda.

He glanced at Brooke. She stared wistfully at the couples shuffling around the floor. Every muscle in his body tensed—in anticipation, no doubt—because he knew what she was going to say even before she opened her mouth.

"I wish I knew how to dance like that."

"Anybody can two-step." He bit his tongue, wishing the words back.

"I can't. Would you teach me, Caleb?"

Ah hell. Now look what he'd gone and done, but it was her birthday. How could he refuse? If he had any luck at all the band would take a long break. "Maybe after dinner."

Right after they gave their orders to the waitress the band left the stage. He hoped his luck would hold, that service would be fast and the band would be slow to return.

"So what do you do, Caleb?"

"Ranch." She waited with an expectant look for him to elaborate. He was reluctant to do so—not because he didn't love what he did, but because most women's eyes glazed over when he started talking about ranch management.

"You?"

She ducked her head and looked at the checkered tablecloth. "I...write."

"Write what? News stuff, travelogues, romances?"

"Self-help books." She got a defensive expression on her face, almost as if she expected him to poke fun at her.

He nodded. "That explains it then."

Her eyes narrowed. "Explains what?"

"All those meaty little phrases you throw out. So who're you helping down here in McMullen county?"

"Myself."

Curious as to what kinds of problems a beautiful

woman like Brooke could have, he arched a brow and waited for her to continue.

She shifted in her seat and confessed, "I'm trying to define my personal success."

There she went again, talking that self-help stuff. The words and delivery were stiff and proper, but there was a yearning in her eyes that told him she was anything but detached. It was kind of cute in a schoolteacherish way. Of course he'd never had any teachers who looked this good.

The waitress arrived with their dinners. Brooke waited for her to leave before asking, "I don't suppose you've ever had to redefine your goals?"

"Can't say that I have. I always knew I'd be ranching."

"Why?"

The smells wafting up from his plate made his mouth water, but it looked like his appetite would have to wait. Back home, when the food hit the table everybody shut up and dug in. He didn't remember many of the manners his momma had tried to teach him before she'd left, but he did remember the one about waiting for the lady at the table to eat first.

"I'm the oldest son of a rancher. Texan born and bred. I'll take over from my dad."

"Do your brothers and sisters feel the same way?" She focused all her attention on him, ignoring the trucker-size barbecue sampler platter in front of her. Either she wanted to try every version the restaurant offered or she had a voracious appetite.

Well, there was another thought he didn't need. Brooke's appetite for food *or anything else* was none of his business. He cleared his throat and tried to remember her question.

"Brothers, three of 'em. And no. One's in medical school, another is—*was*—a world champion bull rider till this year when he up and got married. Patrick's the only one still at home."

"So you had choices, and you chose ranching."

Caleb traced a finger along the outside seam of his jeans. Growing up it hadn't felt like he had choices. He'd felt trapped. It wasn't until Amanda had tried to make him leave Crooked Creek and move to the city that he'd discovered how much he loved the ranch. But how could he explain the love of open spaces and the desire to pit himself against nature to a city gal? His ex hadn't understood, and she'd grown up on a neighboring property.

"Sweetheart, you'd best dig in while it's hot."

Brooke daintily lifted a rib and nibbled on it. Her tongue peeked out to swipe a smear of sauce from her lips. She looked from the coating on her fingers to the fragile paper napkin and back.

"Lick 'em."

"Excuse me?"

"Lick the sauce from your fingers."

She hesitated a moment, then glanced around to see that the other patrons were doing the same. Inserting a finger in her mouth, she sucked off the sauce—one finger at a time then moved on to the next rib.

Oh man. Watching the woman eat was an erotic experience. He probably would've been better off to let her keep talking. He swallowed hard, amazed that she had him so distracted he could barely taste his food. "What about you? How do you go about redefining yourself? Sounds painful."

She smiled. "It can be. The journey of self-discovery is always a bumpy road."

"Not interested in whatever it is your parents do?"

She shuddered. "No. Both are tenured college professors. They write endless theses that no one other than their colleagues can understand. It doesn't matter how brilliant their work is because so few read it. I want to reach masses of people and help them fulfill their potential."

He shifted in his seat. That was the same argument his ex had used. She'd wanted him *to fulfill his potential* by running for office in the county cattlemen's association, then on the state level. She'd even talked about him being the next Texan president, for crying out loud. All the while she planned to paint her nails, spend his money and play queen of the castle. Problem was Crooked Creek wasn't any damned castle, and it had taken her less than two years to blow through every dime his family had saved. Not only had his brother Brand lost his college fund, but they'd had to sell a piece of the ranch to keep from losing the whole thing.

"Does most of your family live nearby?" She nibbled and licked. He had to quit watching her and focus on his own dinner if he wanted to be able to string sentences together coherently.

"All but Cort, the youngest. He's in North Carolina."

"You have roots." She sounded envious. "I'm working on that."

The band returned as the waitress brought Brooke's dessert.

He hated to see the band come back, but he sure was glad the music made it difficult for her to ask her probing questions. The lead singer warbled out a song about a man falling in love and knowing he'd screw it up because he'd done so with every other relationship in his life. Caleb tried to tune it out. It hit a little too close to home. His own relationships tended to be brief because most women didn't want to play second fiddle to ten thousand acres of dirt and four-legged critters. It was only a matter of time before he missed some so-called important date because one of his animals got itself in trouble.

Brooke closed her lips around a forkful of some chocolate concoction, closed her eyes and moaned softly. He wasn't a man prone to imagining things, but his mind immediately connected that sweet sound with sex. Would Brooke look that delirious with a man inside her? Would she close her eyes and tilt back her head, baring her throat to her lover's mouth the way she did now? His gaze traced the slender line of pale skin, finding the pulse beating steadily at the base. His groin throbbed in tandem. He drained his glass of iced tea, hoping the chilled liquid would cool him off.

Brooke swallowed. The pink tip of her tongue appeared and stole a crumb from the corner of her lips. "You should try this. It's positively sinful."

Yep, sin was what he was thinking about—her mouth with something besides that fork in it.

"Sweetheart, a man would be a fool to get between you and your chocolate. You go right ahead and finish every last bite." And torture him to death doing it.

She scooped up a portion and offered it to him. "Try it. I promise you've never tasted anything this good."

Caleb studied her deep green eyes and wondered if she were making a pass. And if he wanted her to be. It didn't seem likely. There was nothing overtly flirtatious about her, but he was so out of practice he could be missing the obvious.

It was no skin off his knuckles if the lady wanted to go slumming. He decided to test her and himself. It wasn't like he had anywhere to be tonight. There were worse ways to pass the midnight hours than in the arms of a beautiful woman—especially one only passing through town. No one would be the wiser if they spent a little time together.

He cupped his hand over hers on the fork and guided the dessert toward his mouth without breaking eye contact. The rich flavor exploded on his tongue. He let his gaze drop to her mouth and imagined tasting the chocolate from her tongue instead of her fork.

Brooke's lips parted on an indrawn breath and her hand trembled within his. When he lifted his gaze to hers again something dark and sultry sparked in her eyes.

His heart—among other things—thudded painfully.

She snatched back the fork, dropped it on the table and looked away. The pulse in her throat fluttered wildly. He didn't miss the nervous way she wet her lips or perched on the edge of her seat as if she were considering making a run for it.

At least the attraction wasn't one-sided.

"Are they two-stepping?" She nodded toward the shuffling couple closest to them. Her breathless voice was about the sexiest thing he'd ever heard.

He jerked his gaze away from the way her rapid breathing shifted her silk shirt across her breasts and eyed the couple plastered close enough to tangle belt buckles. "Nope."

"What do you call it then?"

"Vertical sex."

Brooke's pink lips dropped open. She blushed and sat back in her chair. She continued watching the other dancers until the color in her cheeks evened out. "Can we dance now?"

"Now's as good a time as any." He hoped he could control himself.

Caleb pulled her onto the floor and into his arms. She was the perfect height to tuck her head beneath his chin if he were so inclined, but her body with its soft, sexy curves, had about as much give as a new fence post. "Loosen up. Two quick steps, two slow steps. Backwards. Slide your feet."

She grimaced. "You're just saying that so I won't step on your toes."

"Planning to?"

"I hope not." She glanced up at him, frowned, and then looked back at their feet, concentrating so intently you'd think she was doing brain surgery. The second time her head clipped his chin Caleb decided he'd had enough.

"Brooke, look at me and let me lead. I won't steer you wrong."

She did as he asked, but the agony in her face told him she wasn't enjoying it. She mouthed the count: quick, quick, slow, slow. He shifted his hand from her shoulder to her hip to guide her better. About halfway through the second song she caught the rhythm and cut loose with such a blinding smile that he nearly tripped.

"There you go."

They circled the room a few times. The more she relaxed, the smaller the gap between them became. He didn't think it was intentional, but the slide of her thighs against his was driving him slam out of his mind. He cleared his throat. "Had enough?"

"I could do this all night." He barely heard the softly voiced comment over the band, but he didn't miss the blissful expression on her face.

There were a few things he'd like to do with Brooke that might take all night. Dancing wasn't one of them. "Brooke." He waited until she tipped her head up and locked her gaze with his. "*I* can't do this all night."

Something in his eyes must have clued her in to the trail his thoughts had taken because she stumbled against him and met the tangible proof of his statement. Her eyes widened then something flared in their depths. She stopped in the middle of the floor, causing other dancers to fork around them.

"I—I wasn't trying to lead you on. I mean… Oh my—This is crazy. I've never… I don't even know you and I want—" She tucked her chin and mashed her lips together.

"What is it you want, Brooke?" His blood headed south and his throat closed up. He could barely get the words out.

"Nothing. Never mind. Let's just finish the song and then we can—" Adorably flustered, she pulled him back into the line of dancers, leading again. He let her because his mind was…elsewhere.

She had to be close to his age, but she still blushed, for crying out loud. Something inside him softened. If she'd been the man-eater he'd originally taken her for back at the bar he'd have probably pushed her away. He'd had enough aggressive women to last him three lifetimes. But this vulnerable, shy side of Brooke reeled him in and turned him on.

He stopped beside their table and bent his head to whisper in her ear. ‘‘Know what I want? I want to see if you taste as sweet as that dessert.’’

The shocked look on her face made him wonder if he'd have to resuscitate her.

Brooke dropped into her chair. Her legs would no longer support her. She'd thought learning the two-step would help her fit into her new home state. Instead dancing left her with a hunger for the taste of another Texas product—the handsome, slow-talking, rough-around-the-edges cowboy across the table.

Hadn't she already done enough bad things to her body tonight by sampling the double chocolate raspberry mousse cake and drinking that vile beer? She didn't need to add a one-night stand to her list of sins.

*A one-night stand.* The idea rippled through her like waves on a pond. She'd never had one—and of course she wouldn't tonight—but dear heavens, he tempted her. Her hands shook when she blotted her face with her napkin. She sipped her water and sucked an ice cube in an effort to cool down. Why had ovulating never affected her this way before? Parts of her tingled like they'd never tingled before. She'd heard of the call of the wild, but she'd certainly never experienced it firsthand. Until now.

Caleb wanted her. The knowledge practically made her pant. She saw the need in his coffee-dark eyes, had felt it in the strength of his touch, and in the searing heat of the erection she'd accidentally encountered.

She'd never been so turned on in her entire life—not even by her former lovers. She'd known each of them for *years* before becoming intimate, and she'd thought she loved each of them. She'd known Caleb less than three hours, and she wanted to tear his clothes off.

The waitress passed and Brooke asked for the bill. Her

voice sounded scratchy, and she was amazed the woman understood her. What would she do once she'd paid for their meal?

She had absolutely no idea.

She'd started the evening wanting to explore the way Caleb made her feel. She hadn't expected the experience to last past dessert. After all, what did she have in common with a man who poked cows—or whatever it was called—for a living?

Did she have the nerve to investigate further? She'd never been sexually adventurous. Repressed is the word one of her lovers had used, and all because she liked to schedule their…encounters weeks in advance. She also had a tendency to tell her partner exactly what she liked, but it wasn't because she was being bossy or picky. She knew what she wanted in a mate. She did intend to spend the rest of her life with this person after all. She had a right to high expectations both in bed and out.

And look where that had led her.

She had three failed love affairs to her credit and tomorrow she had the appointment in Dallas with a paternity Popsicle. Her stomach tightened, forcing her to dig in her purse for the roll of antacids. The day after being inseminated she'd fly to California to arrange the shipping of all her belongings from her apartment to her new home in southwestern McMullen County. She'd never see Caleb again.

The emptiness in her stomach was a new experience.

Perhaps it was time to be spontaneous. Renting the Miata was a baby step compared to what she was actually considering. She popped a chalky tablet into her mouth and washed it down.

"Barbecue too spicy?" The genuine concern in his voice and on his face was both unexpected and touching.

"No, I take these for the calcium." And for the baby she hoped to conceive.

"Gonna finish your dessert?"

She'd only taken one bite. Caleb had shared the other and killed her appetite for her beloved chocolate with one steamy look. "I...no. I'll take it with me."

*Start as you mean to go.* Book one, chapter one. She'd spent the last ten years chasing success, trying to please her publisher, her accountant, and her parents. She'd focused on external goals—visible signs of success—rather than internal ones. It left her feeling empty, like a fraud who didn't practice what she preached. When a rival had called her a sellout on a national radio show, she'd acknowledged that he might have a point and vowed to change her focus. The move to Texas signified a shift toward satisfying her emotional needs.

*Right now she needed Caleb.* Oh dear.

She could tell him goodbye, go back to her motel room and finish this milestone birthday alone, or she could reach beyond her comfort zone and test her resolve to find herself.

Be spontaneous. She suppressed a shudder. Spontaneity went against every fiber of her being.

She needed her Day Planner and a pen. It was vital to consider all the angles before making a decision as important as this one. But she'd left her planner in her car, and if she took the time to get it and map a strategy this opportunity would pass.

*Personal growth is only achieved by stepping beyond one's boundaries. Never let a day go by without taking a step toward your goal.* Book one, chapter two.

"M-my motel is just down the road."

He blinked those lush lashes, one slow sweep of black against his tanned skin, but not before she saw desire ignite in his eyes. Caleb leaned forward and she caught her breath, but instead of kissing her like she thought he would—like she'd hoped he would—he pulled out his wallet and tossed enough money on the table to cover the bill.

"I'm supposed to pay for dinner," she protested.

"You can buy the condoms. Lady's choice. Let's go."

When he put it like that she wondered if she might have been precipitous in making her decision.

"I—I—" Her bottom might as well be glued to the chair, and even though she made her living as a public speaker, she couldn't seem to think of a single thing to say.

He paused, his face carefully neutral. "Or I can walk you to your car and point you in the direction of your motel."

*You run out of chances when you stop taking them.* Her own words haunted her. She took a deep breath, wet her lips and tried to summon her courage.

Caleb lifted his hat from the extra chair and set it on his head. His expression tightened. "How about I thank you for your company and say good night right here?"

"No, I—" Her mouth was as dry as the Mojave Desert. She swallowed, but it didn't help. "Caleb, wait."

She'd never been tempted to sleep with a total stranger. Of course, she'd never been impregnated by a man she'd never seen before, either, but she would be tomorrow.

*Be spontaneous.*

Every muscle in her body clenched as she prepared to take the leap. She might as well have been jumping out of an airplane for all the trepidation she felt. "You'll have to tell me where we can buy the…condoms. I'm not familiar with the stores here."

Fire, hot enough to incinerate her where she sat, flashed in Caleb's eyes. "There's a pharmacy on the corner."

Her parents would say she was suffering from a psychosis. Such impulsive behaviors were certainly a deviation from her norm. But her parents would be wrong. Before she reached her room she'd regain control of her emotions and the situation. But first, she had to get her shaky legs to support her. She wobbled to her feet. "Lead the way."

He pressed his palm against her spine and escorted her

out of the restaurant and across the street to the pharmacy. The heat of his touch transferred through her silk jacket, warming her skin and weakening her knees with the promise of more intimate contact to come.

The pharmacy was a small mom and pop operation. She spotted her latest book on a rack near the back, but didn't venture over to sign it because Caleb followed one pace behind. She probably wouldn't have been able to hold the pen anyway.

Brooke snatched the first box of condoms from the shelf and shoved them across the counter to the cashier, hoping she didn't look as mortified as she felt. Then she looked at her purchase. *Oh dear heavens, she'd picked up the jumbo-size box of extra larges.*

Caleb said nothing during the purchase, but he arched a dark brow and rocked back on his boot heels when she found the nerve to meet his amused gaze outside the store. "Ambitious, aren't you?"

Brooke wanted to crawl through the cracks in the sidewalk. She'd never bought condoms before, and frankly, it was embarrassing, but she refused to give up ground by admitting she might have been...overzealous in her purchase.

*Cross those self-imposed boundaries and seize the momentum.*

She stiffened her spine and stared right back. "Afraid you won't live up to my expectations, Caleb?"

A slow and devastatingly sexy smile eased its way across his face. "Sweetheart, I'll do my best or die trying."

Every cell in her body quivered like Jell-O. Oh. My. God. She was actually going to do this. "My motel is—" Her throat knotted and she couldn't finish it.

Caleb had no such problem. "Around the corner." He winked. "Only one in town. The question is whether or not you want my truck parked outside your room."

The gesture was unbelievably considerate considering

she'd picked the man up in a bar and didn't intend to see him again once she checked out of the motel.

He tucked her hair behind her ear and tilted up her chin. The gentle scrape of his fingertip along her jawline was unbearably intimate. ''Why don't you tell me your room number? I'll park across the street at the waffle shop and meet you there.''

She'd reached the point of no return, but the turbulence in her stomach didn't call for an antacid. The only cure was a dark-haired, dark-eyed cowboy. ''Room 118. It's in the back.''

He walked her to her car, opened the door and bent in the opening after she sat down. His arm brushed her breasts as he fastened her seat belt. It was a slow, deliberate move that nearly caused her to have a meltdown right there on the leather upholstery.

''If you change your mind, don't answer the door. No hard feelings.'' He closed her door and walked off before she could think of a reply.

Whether he wanted to admit it or not, Caleb had a mile-wide gallant streak.

If she had to take a walk outside her comfort zone, at least she was doing so with someone she believed she could trust.

The question was could she trust *herself?*

# Three

Caleb didn't expect Brooke to answer the door when he knocked. He figured she'd come to her senses once she was out of range of the attraction flaring between them and decide not to waste herself on a lowly cowboy. And he wouldn't let himself be disappointed.

He rapped once and she eased the door open. She'd kicked off her shoes. Her painted toenails dug into the carpet, and her teeth dug into her lip. ''Come in.''

Judging by the way his body saluted her husky voice and bare feet the show would be over quicker than he could hog-tie a steer. He needed to slow things down. So even though he wanted to toss her on that motel mattress, bury himself inside her and ride like the wind, he rocked back on his heels, hooked his thumbs through his belt loops, and said, ''Make me.''

Her eyes widened and her lips parted in surprise. ''Excuse me?''

''If you want me, city girl, come and get me.''

She looked left and right down the deserted walkway, but in this back corner of the motel they were the only ones around. She folded her arms across her chest. "I thought you were a big, tough cowboy who knew exactly what you wanted."

He winked. "You got part of that right."

Her gaze dropped to his distended fly. She blushed and looked away. Her nostrils flared and her breasts rose as she drew in a deep, shaky breath. He was beginning to think he'd chosen the wrong strategy when she peeked at him from beneath her lashes. The spark in her eyes combined with a sensuous curving of her lips sent a jolt through him.

Very deliberately, Brooke untied the silk belt knotted at her waist. Caleb's pulse leaped and only raced faster as she eased the strip of fabric inch-by-inch through her belt loops. Once it was free she pulled it taut between her hands and ever so slowly twisted the ends around her palms. Every adolescent fantasy he'd ever had came rushing back.

She arched the slip of fabric up and over his hat. Cool and slick, it curved around his nape. She tugged him into the room one step at a time.

He'd challenged her, but he hadn't expected such an enthusiastic response. He wanted to kick the door closed and grind his lips and body against hers. It nearly killed him to wait for her next move.

Without breaking eye contact, she transferred both ends of the tether to one hand, freeing the other to remove his hat and place it on the table beside the door. His heart nearly knocked a hole through his chest when she pursed her lips and considered him from his boots to his eyebrows.

"I've never done this before," she confessed in a whisper and shut the door.

It was difficult to think with her soft fingertip tracing his bottom lip, but surely at her age she didn't mean what he thought she meant. He opened his mouth and tried to taste her but she'd moved on to tease his ear.

"Which this? Making love or tying a man in knots?"

Her quiet laugh drifted over him like a cool breeze on bare, damp skin. "Am I tying you in knots, Caleb?"

"Yes, ma'am."

She tugged on her belt, pulling his head down and positioning his lips at a reachable height. His mouth watered, anticipating her taste. To keep from grabbing her he gripped his belt loops so tight his thumbs went numb.

Her breath fanned his lips, but at the last minute she veered left and kissed his jaw. Her lips were soft, cool and dry. He could rectify that and have her hot and wet—inside and out—in seconds, but he waited, determined to let her set the pace even if it killed him. And it might. But he'd rather be dead than go off like a misfired cannon. He wondered if mentally calculating feed ratios would cool him down.

She nibbled along his jaw, dipping the tip of her slick tongue in the cleft of his chin. His knees nearly buckled. He swallowed, but a knot the size of an armadillo stayed stuck in his throat.

She drew back a fraction, aligning her mouth with his once more. "I've never made love to a man I wasn't committed to."

Alarmed, he drew back. His mother had been a cheater. He would never be the one responsible for breaking up a family. "You're not married, are you?"

"No." She sounded a little disappointed. "You're currently the only man in my life, and that's just for tonight. You understand? Afterward we say goodbye and forget this ever happened."

Usually he was the one to make his intentions clear upfront. It felt a little funny to be on the receiving end. Even though he agreed they had no future, he sure as hell didn't intend to be forgettable. "Fine by me, but I want all night, not just one go'round."

She shivered. "All right. How does one go about a one-night stand, Caleb? I don't know what to do next."

Oh man, did he ever have suggestions, but he was game for whatever she dished out. "Anything you want, sweetheart."

She tugged on the silk. "Should I tie you up or will you be a good boy?"

The look she shot him from beneath her lashes nearly caused a problem he hadn't had since his first time. He tensed every muscle and fought for control. Sweat popped out on his forehead and his throat closed up like somebody had put a noose around it. His chest was tight and he could barely breathe. "I'll be good whether you tie me up or not."

Tingling in every inch of her body, Brooke drew back in surprise. She'd made the absurd remark half-hoping she'd frighten Caleb away. The men in her life had always tried to dominate her in bed and out, and control wasn't something she handed over easily. Ask any of her former lovers. More than once she'd suspected her inability to let go had contributed to her unsatisfactory sex life. Caleb, on the other hand, seemed willing to let her lead.

"You mean you'd let me?"

Although he shrugged casually, his heart pounded harder and faster beneath her palm. "Don't see why not. Hadn't tried it before. Might be fun."

Desire had never, ever affected her so strongly that she trembled with anticipation for what would follow. Caleb made her yearn to experiment in ways that had never tempted her before. She mentally shuffled through every sexual act she'd ever been curious about and never had the nerve to try and wondered if she was brave enough to explore the forbidden with a man she'd never see again.

No. Even though there was safety in anonymity, she was more of a navigator than an adventurer. She liked to know where she was going and how she'd get there.

*But you'll never see him again,* her conscience insisted.

"Sweetheart?" He interrupted her search for explanations.

"Hmm?"

"I don't mean to be pushy here, but could we move along?" The huskiness of his voice told her that she wasn't the only one fighting overpowering need.

"You have somewhere to go, cowboy?"

He gave a rough laugh. "*Going* wasn't what I had in mind."

Cupping one big hand around her nape, he traced her bottom lip with his thumb. The rasp of his skin over her flesh made her quiver. His coffee-dark gaze practically scalded her and his grin was lethal. "I have a hunger for your mouth that just won't quit. I'm wondering how long you're gonna make me wait before you put me out of my misery."

"My—oh." She couldn't catch her breath. Her past partners never talked *during*. If Caleb talked it might distract her from her goal. It took all her concentration to—to— He lowered his head until his mouth hovered a centimeter from hers and she lost her train of thought.

"Are you gonna make me suffer, city girl?" His breath fanned her lips, making her heart race like she'd never been kissed.

She yanked the belt, closing the gap between them. Heat seared her the moment their lips touched. From belt buckle to nose, he burned her. She brushed her mouth over his once, twice. Impatient. Hungry. Cautious.

The need to let go and see where the current of desire would carry her coursed through her, but if she wanted to get any pleasure out of this, she had to stay in control and focused on the outcome.

Caleb's hand clenched in her hair. A groan rumbled in his throat and vibrated through her. Feeling bolder, she sucked his full, lower lip into her mouth and teased the silky inside. He made an impatient sound, but didn't pounce. She wondered what it would take to push him over the edge. The determination to find his limits filled her, but that would have to wait until she was sufficiently aroused or she'd be left out.

She traced her tongue along his teeth. He drew a sharp breath, widened his stance and settled his hands on her hips. If the hot length of each of his fingers could arouse her this much through her silk suit she wondered how she'd survive when he touched bare skin. Eager to find out, she cupped his strong jaw with both hands and traced his cheekbones with her thumbs, and then deepened the kiss, tentatively exploring further.

Caleb startled her by sucking her tongue and pulling rhythmically on her body the way she'd pull on his later when he was inside her—if she was lucky. A thrill shivered over her.

An impatience to investigate every inch of him enveloped her, but she held back. Her past encounters had been a race to completion, which she often hadn't finished. Her only chance of finding satisfaction lay in keeping the pace slow enough for her body to warm up. It took her an embarrassingly long time.

Although Caleb seemed to have given her a head start tonight.

Closing her eyes, she inhaled deeply, savoring the scent of aroused man and a hint of aftershave. Blindly she explored the width and firmness of his chest, the trimness of his waist and the tautness of his belly above the thick leather belt while she sampled his mouth, his neck, his ears. The first two snaps of his Western-style shirt were already unfastened. She popped open three more and stroked his hot skin. Crisp hair teased her palms, shooting need to her very core.

"Caleb—" All night she'd wondered how his hands would feel on her belly and breasts, and she couldn't wait another moment to find out.

"Tell me what you want." His voice rumbled against her cheek. His lips feathered over her cheekbone.

She'd never been a vocal lover. Covering his hands with hers, she slid them upward and whispered, "I want you to touch me."

As if he'd been waiting for those words, he yanked her closer. One hand splayed on her buttock, holding her captive against the length of his body. The other tangled in her hair. He captured her mouth in a ravenous kiss.

Alarm shot through her. The balance of power had shifted. He would race onward and leave her to finish in a frustrated last place. She wanted to ask him to slow down. Her finicky body had certain requirements, but the way he devoured her mouth didn't leave room for conversation or even coherent thought.

He danced her backward until the wall pressed her spine. Sandwiched between the cool solid surface and hard heat of his body, she couldn't move. Her hands were trapped uselessly between them. He thrust his thigh between hers, applying sweet pressure to her most sensitive spot. For a moment she battled a shameless urge to slide against him, but the move seemed too brazen, and it wasn't something she'd done before. She managed to restrain herself, but it wasn't easy.

His hands skimmed over her in the lightest of caresses. Teasing. Tantalizing. Her clothes provided no barrier to the patterns he traced over her waist, her thighs, and along her spine. All the while he did things to her mouth that no man had ever done before. Kissing had never been particularly exciting for her. It seemed to be something her partners enjoyed much more than she did, but Caleb seemed determined to introduce her to what she'd been missing. *And she liked it.*

Her breasts ached for his attention. If she could have freed her hands she would have grabbed his and put them where she needed his touch the most. After all, she knew she required quite a bit of foreplay there to get things started.

As if sensing her thoughts, his hands plunged beneath

her blouse. She gasped, nearly sucking the breath from his lungs. His callused palms lightly scraped her waist, leaving a trail of goose bumps in their wake. She shivered despite the furnace heat of his body and the blasts of his scorching breath on her cheek.

In agonizingly slow motion he eased his thumbs beneath the elastic band of her bra, gliding them backward and forward. His thumbnails scraped the sensitive skin on the underside of her breasts, and her nipples tingled in anticipation. Hunger built in her midsection. She wanted to groan in frustration when he bypassed the sensitive tips to bisect her belly with the rasp of a fingernail. Her stomach muscles quivered.

He moved to the waistband of her skirt, and with a deft flick of his fingers the button gave way. The zipper quickly followed. And still he kissed her, with silken strokes of his tongue and teasing nibbles of his teeth. It was too much. It wasn't enough. He made her needy in an unfamiliar way.

He eased back a few inches and cool air swept between them. Before she could pull him back her skirt puddled at her ankles. Now that he'd freed her mouth she wanted to protest, to slow him down, but when his hand splayed over her belly, a finger edging beneath the band of her panties, the words incinerated on her lips.

He held her at arms' length and groaned. "Should've known."

She shook her head, trying to clear the sensual haze. "Should have known what?"

"That you wouldn't wear white cotton. You're determined to drive me outta my mind, aren't you, city girl?" He skated a knuckle along her jaw and his lips curved in a slow, sensual smile that sent adrenaline surging through her veins.

He dropped to his knees and pressed a kiss against her lacy, lavender panties. His breath steamed her through the thin fabric and sent her senses reeling. She clutched his shoulders for support. Caleb was moving too fast and doing things all out of her usual order. She opened her mouth to tell him what she liked and how she liked it, but the words vanished when he stripped her panties with a quick jerk and brushed his lips against her curls.

Her breath caught at the boldness of his actions and at the strength of her reaction to them. He'd skipped all the preliminaries. There was a certain order to this business that ought to be respected. She shouldn't be enjoying this, but she was. He hadn't even touched her breasts. Being so out of control frightened her. Intent on yanking him back up, she curled her fingers into his thick hair.

In her mind she knew she wasn't ready for Caleb's primitive brand of loving, but the sensations coursing through her body argued otherwise. He gently stroked her with his hands and mouth, coaxing a response from her. She knew she needed to tell him...*something,* but it took all her concentration to keep her knees from buckling.

Caleb freed one foot and then the other from her skirt and panties then curled his hands around her ankles and eased them apart. He stoked upward in torturously slow circles—the same tantalizing circles his tongue drew on her sensitive flesh. The sudden rush of pleasure made her dizzy.

Her libido galloped ahead, as if it hadn't spent the last fifteen years plodding toward satisfaction, most often not getting there. Her muscles trembled. Her chest and belly tightened. Her tenuous hold on her control ebbed.

This couldn't be happening. She never, *ever,* reached the pinnacle with less than thirty minutes of serious foreplay, including substantial attention above the waist—primarily the seduction of her mind. But here she was. Digging into a stranger's scalp and holding on for dear life as she spontaneously combusted. *She,* who never did anything spontaneously, exploded like a shaken bottle of champagne.

Warmth rushed over her in waves. Her legs quivered

like a tuning fork. Her body hummed and she couldn't catch her breath. What in the world had just happened here? What had the man done to her?

"Where are the condoms?" Caleb pulled her from her cloud of disbelief. He stood in front of her. The tense expression on his face said they weren't finished yet. Her heart rate tripled. Wordlessly she pointed to the bedside table.

He ripped open the box, withdrew a foil packet and stuck it between his teeth. In two strides he stood in front of her again. She watched in amazement as he wasted no time unbuckling his belt and jeans. Pulling the condom from his teeth, he cupped her chin, pressed a hard, quick kiss on her lips and stared deep into her eyes. "The first time is going to be fast. I'll make it up to you."

Before she could make sense of his words, he'd shoved his pants to his knees and rolled the protection over a thick erection. "Wrap your legs around my waist and hold on tight, sweetheart."

She should protest that she'd never been able to enjoy quickies, but her body hummed and throbbed for his possession, belying her thoughts. His words and touch built an unfamiliar hunger inside her that she wanted to explore.

He lifted her as if she weighed no more than a doll and pressed her back against the wall. Afraid of being dropped, she wrapped her arms around his neck. Caleb cupped her buttocks and hitched her legs around his waist. He filled her with one deep thrust and she cried out in ecstasy. *She,* who never made a sound during coupling, cried out in delight as he filled her.

Caleb hammered into her like a man racing out of control, but for the first time in her life, Brooke found herself keeping pace. He nibbled her neck, her ear, and then captured her mouth. His kiss mimicked the motion of his body until breathless, they broke the kiss to gasp for air.

She lost herself in the passion darkening his eyes and

couldn't look away. No man had ever looked at her like her very being was essential to his surviving the next few moments. It was a heady, empowering feeling to know that she'd put that hunger in Caleb's eyes. *She'd* caused the sweat to dampen his skin. *She* was the one who'd caused his cheeks to flush and his breath to pant.

In wonder, she found herself climbing the peak again and tumbling over. *And the man had never even touched her breasts.*

He groaned against her neck. His breath scorched her skin. She felt him shudder and penetrate even deeper. Off she went again. *She,* who never found satisfaction multiple times erupted in rapture *again.*

Stunned and sated by a capacity for pleasure she hadn't known she possessed, she depended solely on Caleb to keep her from falling, and *she* who never depended on anyone but herself, hung on the man like a string of lights on a Christmas tree.

Caleb staggered backward until his knees hit the mattress. His legs couldn't support the two of them anymore, but he wasn't ready to turn Brooke loose yet. He liked the way she'd melted all over him, clinging like a vine on a wire fence.

He fell backward, bouncing on the bed. Brooke bounced on top of him, and he groaned as her body gripped his in slick heat. For several moments he lay there trying to catch his breath, trying to figure out how he could have been so crass as to take the woman against a wall when they had a comfortable bed in the room. If she'd had a low opinion of cowboys before, this hadn't helped.

"What did you do to me?" She sounded indignant.

Embarrassed that he'd gone off like a Roman candle with a short fuse, he tightened his arms around her. Next time, he'd show a little finesse. He might even manage to get their clothes off first. "If you don't know then I didn't do it right. Maybe we'd better try again."

She shifted, and his blood herded right back to the corral where she had his horse penned. His thirty-eight-year-old body obviously didn't know it needed time to recover. The woman was stronger than a narcotic and just as addictive. Skating a hand down her stiff spine, he cupped the soft skin of her bottom and held her close.

"You don't understand. That wasn't me."

He didn't understand why she sounded so worried. "Sure feels like you to me." He shifted his hips, reminding her they were still joined beneath the hem of her shirt.

Her breath caught. Her eyes closed. She sat up straighter, her smooth legs still straddling his.

"You don't understand. I don't—I'm not—" She licked her swollen lips, making him realize he might have been a little too rough. She had a bad case of whisker burn. "I'm not the wild woman you just..."

"Made love with." He finished her sentence because he didn't think she would—at least not in complimentary words. "And, sweetheart, if that wasn't you making those purring noises, then these walls are thinner than I thought, and your neighbors are having as much fun as we are."

Her cheeks pinked and she tried to scramble off him. He grabbed her thighs. "Whoa now, go slow. We don't want to spill our cargo. You said yourself that tonight was it. Don't want to risk consequences."

And dammit, that wasn't regret tightening his chest.

Horrified, Brooke eased off Caleb. She'd spent months searching for the ideal sperm donor. The last thing she wanted to do was to end up being accidentally inseminated by a man she knew nothing about. A man she'd picked up in a bar. Oh dear.

He looked from her to the mirror and back then whistled through his teeth. "Now *that* is sexy."

She glanced back to see what had him so impressed. The pale globes of her bottom played peekaboo with the back hem of her jacket. She could only imagine what it left bare in the front. Embarrassed and feeling suddenly shy now that the haze of passion had waned, she crossed her hands in front of herself.

Grinning, he shook his head and stood. Caleb tipped her chin with one hand and cupped her waist with the other. "Too late to hide now. I know how you taste."

She couldn't think of a single reply to such an intimate comment. Every fiber of her being hummed from the intimacy of how and where he'd tasted her.

He dipped his head until his lips were a whisper away from hers. "I want you again, Brooke, but this time I want you naked. Hell, I want us both naked."

Her body—the one previously labeled unresponsive—tingled with renewed awareness as he turned toward the bathroom.

She heard the shower turn on and sagged against the dresser, hoping she could regain her equilibrium while he was out of sight.

What had she done? What had he done? And how could she want to do it again?

"Brooke." Naked, Caleb stood in the doorway. His beautifully carved cheekbones paled in comparison to the perfection of the rest of his muscled frame. His shoulders were tanned and broad, and his hips trim and pale. The wide triangle of dark hair covering his chest arrowed down over his flat abdomen to a denser crop surrounding his semiaroused shaft. His long legs were thickly muscled and strong enough that he'd borne her weight while making love.

Her stomach fluttered and her mouth dried. Could she actually *enjoy* such primitive coupling? Surely not.

He crooked his finger and her heart sprinted like a thoroughbred bursting out of the gate. He wanted her to join him. "I don't—I've never showered with a man."

He strolled toward her, stopping just inches away. Reaching for the button at the hem of her jacket, he released it and then worked his way upward until he'd opened the last one. With a flick of fingers he unhooked the front closure of her bra and cupped her breasts with his callused hands. The sensation of warm rough palms on her sensitive flesh was both too much and not enough. When his thumbnails scraped over her nipples she nearly collapsed at his feet in a puddle of need.

"This is your day for firsts, isn't it? Come on, Brooke. Let me get you wet."

His gaze scorched her and then he turned and headed for the bathroom. He paused in the doorway, glancing back over his shoulder and beckoned her to follow wherever he led.

And she did.

Awareness crept slowly through the cloud of exhaustion cocooning her. As far as a journey of self-discovery went, Brooke couldn't imagine taking a more enjoyable one than the one she'd shared with Caleb.

She smiled at the man sleeping sprawled beside her in the bed. Last night he'd shown her erogenous zones she'd never seen on any map, and he'd taught her things about herself that even at thirty-five she hadn't known.

Her body was tired, pleasantly achy and totally sated for the first time in her life. With Caleb she hadn't been cold or unresponsive. With every touch and every look, he'd made her feel like a sex goddess—which she most definitely was not. Remembering last night would make today's procedure tolerable.

Punctual to a fault—or so one of her former boyfriends had said—she often woke before her alarm sounded. She rolled over to check the time, but the alarm clock wasn't on the bedside table. Something about the clock niggled at her memory. She jolted upright, and then she saw it, lying across the room against the door. In pieces.

The memory of the cord tangling around her ankle during a particularly acrobatic maneuver rushed back at her, heating her. Caleb had extricated her and pitched the clock. She'd been a wild woman.

Jumping out of bed, she didn't even bother to drag the sheet with her as she normally would have. *No, normally she would have carefully laid her robe at the end of the bed the night before in preparation for the awkward morning after.*

But there'd been nothing *normal* about last night—at least not in her books.

"Where you headed in such a hurry?" Sleep roughened Caleb's voice. He grabbed her hand before she could escape.

"I need to know what time it is. Our watches are in the bathroom."

He squinted toward the window. Sunlight leaked around the closed curtains. "'Bout nine. Maybe ten. Come'ere."

He had to be wrong, otherwise…

She didn't want to think about otherwise.

"I can't." But the temptation to crawl back into bed with him nearly overwhelmed her. "I have a plane to catch. I have an appointment in Dallas."

He released her, but she saw reluctance in his eyes. Racing to the bathroom, she dug through the towels strewn over the counter. *She never threw towels on the counter.* Finally she found her watch. And shrieked.

Nine thirty-seven.

Wide-eyed and gloriously naked, Caleb jerked to a halt in the bathroom door. "What's'it?"

"My flight leaves in twenty-three minutes. I'm going to miss it. And if I miss my flight I'll miss my appointment."

He scratched his bare belly, drawing her attention to his morning arousal. She tried unsuccessfully to block the memory of the texture and taste of his skin from her thoughts.

He shrugged. "So catch a later one and reschedule."

She shoved her fingers through her hair and tugged. "I can't. The airport is an hour from here. My flight is at ten o'clock and my appointment at the clinic is at noon. It's the last one of the day before the doctor goes on vacation for three weeks.

*"I'm going to miss my appointment."* Overwhelmed by the enormity of her latest failure, she sank down on the edge of the tub. The cold porcelain reminded her that she was naked. She should have been embarrassed, but as Caleb had pointed out more than once during the night, it was a little late for modesty considering she'd done things to this man and with this man that she hadn't even tried with the men she'd thought she wanted to marry.

He knelt in front of her with an expression of genuine concern on his face. "So we'll get you an appointment with a doc here in Tilden."

"No, you don't understand—" And she wouldn't explain. Her decision to be inseminated was a private one and now, a moot one.

He tipped up her chin. A frown puckered his forehead. "Nothing's wrong is it?"

"You're not going to catch anything, if that's what you're anxious about."

He swore and stood. "That's not what I meant. We covered all that last night, and we used protection each time. I was worried about you."

She couldn't remember the last time she'd cried, but his concern made her eyes burn fiercely. She blinked rapidly.

"Hey, none of that." He pulled her into his arms and cradled her against his chest.

The rasp of his fingers up and down her spine, combined with the hard, hot press of his body chased her tears away. Even in the midst of a disaster she felt the tingle of need, but she tamped it down. Her walk on the wild side was over.

How could she make a man who knew exactly what he was going to do with his life understand that goals were her life, her livelihood? Missing one meant jeopardizing the other. She couldn't. All she could do was try to end this with her dignity intact. "I'll call the airline and the doctor's office and see what I can do."

"There you go." He nuzzled her temple and pressed a kiss on her brow. The hair on his chest teased her with featherlight touches.

Her body ignited. "I…you should probably leave."

"Probably should. You going to be okay?"

Forcing a smile she didn't feel to her lips, she nodded.

"Guess I'll get dressed then. If you insist." He arched a brow, his expression hopeful.

"I'm sorry. I have…"

"It's okay, Brooke." He left her in the bathroom.

She splashed water on her face and searched for a positive slant to the horrendous situation. It worried her that she—the queen of optimism—was too shaken to find one. Pulling her robe from the hook behind the door, she tied it around herself and stepped into the bedroom. At the very least Caleb deserved her thanks and a polite goodbye.

"For a city gal, you aren't half bad."

Surprised, she stopped in her tracks and met his dark gaze. "*Really.* Well, for a cowboy you're—"

"Damned good." He looked up from the belt he'd just fastened. His teasing grin nearly brought her to her knees.

She choked on a laugh. "Yes. Well, um. Thank you for making my birthday special."

"My pleasure, ma'am." He closed the gap between them until he stood so close she could feel the warmth radiating from him. "And I mean it. Matter of fact, if you weren't in such a hurry I'd suggest we do this again."

Temptation nipped at her. "Against my better judgment I'd probably agree."

"Probably? Sweetheart, there ain't no probably to it. If we both didn't have to be someplace else I'd have you outta that robe and beggin' in thirty seconds." He smoothed a hand over her hair and tucked a wayward strand behind her ear. He lingered, tracing a path to the pulse pounding at the base of her neck. "Just like you did last night. I love that little noise you make."

Heat filled her cheeks and other places not so obvious now that she had her robe on. If you could bottle this man he'd be called temptation. "No, we wouldn't because...I'm not like that."

"Not like what?" He pressed a kiss against her forehead.

"I don't—I never—I just don't do what I did last night."

"Sweetheart, you did it more'n a dozen times."

She wanted to hide in the closet. "I—you were counting!"

He chuckled. "Oh, yeah. Weren't you?"

She was ashamed to admit that she had been. Thank goodness she'd never have to face the man across the boardroom table and pretend she hadn't become insatiable in his arms.

"Thank you for a memorable night."

He reached for his wallet and pulled out a business card. "Like I said, we were careful, but if you have any problems, give me a call."

She took the card without looking at it. She didn't want to know Caleb's last name or where he was from because she had no intention of calling him or seeing him after today.

Prolonging their relationship would only disappoint him in the long run. After getting dumped by three lovers—two of whom had cheated on her—she knew she didn't have whatever it took to hold a man's interest.

Caleb pulled on his hat when she said nothing else. "Goodbye, Brooke, and thanks for turning a real loser of a day around for me. I'll stop by the office and pay for the clock."

"You don't have to—" The door closed on her words.

Before she could give in to the temptation to see how close Caleb lived to her new home she raced to the bathroom, shredded his card and flushed it down the toilet. Just knowing he was in the same state would be torture enough.

The last thing she needed as she began her new approach to life was the lure of a dead-end detour. She and the cowboy had nothing in common. She was aiming for the stars and his feet were firmly planted on the ground.

# Four

"So who was she?" Patrick called from his seat on the top rail of the corral fence.

Caleb looked at his brother over the saddle he'd just settled on the back of his horse. "Who was who?"

"The one who put the hickey on your neck."

He was too damned old to be blushing, and he'd never been the type to kiss and tell—probably because Patrick, although two years younger, could have topped anything he had to say anyway. His brother was a star player—in the sport of women. "It's a rash."

Patrick laughed. "Yeah. I've used that one before, but a rash doesn't keep a smile on your face for nearly a week and you haven't quit smiling since you got home. Do I know her?"

"You mean have you slept with her? I doubt it."

Patrick's grin broadened and Caleb realized he'd revealed more than he intended.

The mare sensed his tension and shuffled nervously. He

stroked her glossy neck and scratched her ears. He'd known from the day he spotted the skittish bay at the livestock sale two years ago that she'd be worth her weight if he could get past her distrust of men. Her previous owner had abused her both mentally and physically. It had taken almost a year to earn her trust, but the effort had been well worth it. As far as he was concerned she was the best mount on the property.

"She lives in Tilden?" Patrick pressed.

"No."

"Well, we both know she's not a local. You haven't dipped your wick in the local beeswax since Amanda claimed to be knocked up. You know, not all women are as conniving as your ex or as unfaithful as Ma. Hey, quit scowling at me. Your mug's ugly enough without twistin' it thataway."

It was a good thing twelve hundred pounds of nervous horseflesh stood between them. Otherwise, he might have punched his brother. He finished adjusting the saddle, hoping Patrick would take his silence as a hint to get lost. He led Rockette outside the corral and mounted up. As soon as he stepped out of the shade of the barn, the sun beat down on him.

Patrick stopped him with a hand on the rein. "You should've told Brand about the auction. He'd have chipped in the extra ten grand you needed."

"Our little brother has bailed me out one time too many already. Besides, he has his hands full with the twins on the way."

Patrick shrugged. "He can afford it."

"It's my debt."

"For ten years you've worked seventy-hour weeks, taking odd jobs all over the county. Life is passing you by, Caleb, while you bust your butt for a piece of land."

"You'd better hope like the dickens the new owner will continue to lease that land to us or we're liable to lose what's left of Crooked Creek. Without those acres we can't run enough head to make a profit."

Patrick looked surprised and no wonder. After a hard day's work he was more likely to spend his free time in the local bar or a barfly's bed than poring over the ranch accounts. "That bad, huh?"

"That bad. I'm heading over there now. The moving vans have cleared out, but the only vehicle I've seen is a sedan. There's not a pickup truck or tractor in sight. I'm hoping the new owner is one of those city folks who likes the idea of a ranch, but not the work or the cattle that go with it."

Patrick groaned. "Or worse, it could be an actor who'll be flying in and out in a helicopter and spooking the herd. Want me to come along?"

The offer was unexpected. Patrick wasn't the type to go hat-in-hand anywhere unless there were single women involved. He must think some Hollywood starlet had bought the place. "I can handle it."

He whistled to his former neighbor's dog. "Let's go see who's living in your house, Rico."

Brooke's heels clicked on the heart-of-pine floors as she wandered around the public areas of her new home. She preferred the large, open rooms to the smaller and darker private quarters.

The previous owners had auctioned off the former dude ranch lock, stock, and barrel, leaving nearly everything behind. It was a little eerie, as if they'd gone out on an errand and might return any moment. She'd inherited magazines and books intended for the dude ranch guests, as well as heavy pine furniture which was so far removed from the glass and cane she'd brought from California she couldn't imagine ever being comfortable on it.

Caleb, on the other hand, would fit perfectly into the rustic décor. She shoved a hand into the hair at her brow and tugged in frustration. It was disgusting how easily *and how frequently* over the last two days she'd pictured him sprawled on the sofa in front of the massive stone fireplace with his boots propped on the scarred coffee table. She'd had the same problem when she'd crawled into the wide timber frame bed at night. He might as well have been right there beside her for all the time she'd spent with him in her dreams and all the sleep she'd missed.

She'd tried without success to limit her memories of their time together to a scant five minutes during lunch when she felt the most able to deal with the twists fate had thrown her, but Caleb kept pushing past the barriers she'd erected. Memories of that night continued to haunt her.

Why, in weak moments, did she wish she hadn't flushed his phone number? She really didn't need to hear his voice. Besides, now that he knew just how much effort it took to arouse her he wouldn't be interested in talking to her anyway. Ask any of her exes. Her inadequacies had driven two of them to seek other lovers.

A satisfied part of her conscience reminded her that it hadn't taken Caleb all that long to engage her usually reluctant body.

She huffed an irritated breath and shoved aside a carton containing her best crystal stemware. It didn't matter how easily he'd pushed her buttons. He was all wrong for her. She had her goals mapped out. There wasn't room for Caleb in her plans even if she knew where to find him. When she did eventually look for a life-mate, he'd have to be an asset to her career not just an asset to her sexual well-being. There was more to life than physical gratification—even if her body craved more of what he'd delivered.

Squelching the memories of a shared hot shower and hotter sheets, she opened a carton containing her china and then closed it again. The cabinets were full of heavy earthenware dishes more fitting to the down-home atmosphere. Her belongings didn't belong in this house, but that would soon change. In the meantime, she'd store her things in the barn with her furniture.

Pouring herself a mug of herbal tea, she sat at the table, pushed aside the topographical map of her property, and opened the folder containing the sperm donor's profile. Now *this* was the man for her—at least on paper—and next month at her rescheduled doctor's appointment their genes would meet.

Pulling forward her Day Planner she made a list of the reasons why this donor was perfect for her. His genetics were impeccable. He wouldn't interfere with her career, leave socks on the floor or the toilet seat up. He wouldn't complain when she had to be out of town or if her gross income contained more digits than his.

He wouldn't bring another lover home to their bed. She underlined that one. Twice.

Shoving aside the negative thoughts, she concentrated on the positives. If everything went according to plan, this absent donor would enrich her life in the most important way. He'd give her the beginnings of the family she craved—a child. She closed her eyes and tried to visualize the baby they'd create, but even though she had both his and her vital statistics a picture refused to form. Instead other thoughts crowded her mind.

Her mystery donor wouldn't haunt her nights or leave her tired, achy and aroused every morning. He wouldn't push her to achieve satisfaction more times in one night than she had in previous *years.*

She pressed her hands to her temples, willing the memories and accompanying restlessness away. She'd never had trouble compartmentalizing her life before, but a brown-eyed cowboy with a crooked smile refused to be cordoned off.

Maybe it was because she was focusing on the theme of her next book. She kept returning to the question of why Caleb had come into her life at this particular time and why she couldn't block thoughts of him from her mind. She wrote: *You can't move forward when you're looking backward.*

The doorbell rang. She grimaced and lay down her pen. The first thing she planned to replace was the "Happy Trails" door chime. Her retreat called for something more…dignified than an old Roy Rogers tune.

Smoothing her hands down the stiff legs of her brand-new pink jeans she opened the door. Her heart stopped. Caleb had stepped right out of her fantasies and onto her welcome mat.

He'd tracked her down.

Her heart resumed beating at a pace so fast it made her head spin. She thought she might possibly hyperventilate. Her memories hadn't done him justice. She'd forgotten how handsome he was. Six feet of solid muscle. And oh what he could do with those muscles. Surely the flush filling her body resulted from embarrassment over the wanton behavior she'd exhibited with him? But she'd never felt the heat of embarrassment *there*.

Why was he here? Had that night not been enough for him, either? She stifled the thought. It *had* been enough and it was over. An aberration never to be repeated again.

"Caleb."

A passion so hot she nearly ignited replaced the surprise in his eyes, and then he scowled. The pleat between his brows matched the cleft in his chin. "What in the hell are you doing here?"

Reality hit her like a silent audience. Cold foreboding filled her belly. He hadn't been looking for her. "I live here. I bought the ranch."

"You—" Anger and disbelief cut off his words. "*You* bought the ranch?"

What was she missing? She couldn't begin to fathom why he'd have such a reaction. Of course, her thoughts were somewhat muddled by the tingling in her breasts and thighs. "Yes."

"Why?"

Was that a trick question? She put a hand to her throat. Her pulse pounded beneath her fingertips. "For my business."

His eyes narrowed. "What kind of business?"

"A retreat."

His broad shoulders relaxed. She wondered if the scratches she'd carved on them in ecstasy had healed. "Good. Then you won't need the pastures."

Pastures? "Caleb, I'm afraid I don't understand. Why are you concerned about my land?"

"I live next door. For the last ten years I've leased acreage from the previous owner for my herd. I need to continue."

Dumbfounded, she stared at the man who'd made her moan like a porn-flick actress. *He lived next door.* Oh. My. God. She didn't have to worry about seeing him across a boardroom table. No, all she had to do to be reminded of the night she'd lost control and loved every minute of it was look over the fence.

She inhaled slowly and struggled for calm and reason. She needed to sit down. "You'd better come in."

The dog beside him whimpered. It was easily the most indiscriminately bred mutt she'd ever seen. He had one blue eye and one brown. One of his ears looked as if it had been gnawed off in a fight, and the poor thing was skinny. She could see his ribs.

"Stay, Rico." The dog lay down with his head on its paws. It turned big, sad eyes in her direction. It was a truly pitiful sight. If she hadn't been having a crisis moment she would have taken a minute to pet it. Instead she turned on her heel. One problem at a time. The biggest one followed her into the room.

She sat in a club chair and sank down until her feet left the floor. Just as she expected, the oversize pieces suited Caleb perfectly. He looked entirely too comfortable in *her* home.

Now what had he asked? Oh, yes. "I can't lease you

the land. I'm going to need it for the swimming pool, tennis courts and driving range."

"You already have a pool and the others won't take more than a few acres," he countered.

"I'm afraid you don't understand. I need peace and tranquillity for my guests to recharge and regroup, and that tiny pool is inadequate."

"I need your pastures to graze my cattle." He sat forward, bracing his hands on his splayed knees. "Whoa. Back up. Guests?"

"Yes."

"You mean friends and family, right?"

"No, I mean clients who pay me for my expertise."

His mouth dropped open. "Pay you… People pay you for those little ditties you're always tossing out?"

She tried not to be insulted. It wasn't easy. "I'll have you know I speak to crowds as large as ten thousand at a time. In addition, corporations hire me to come in and address their executives. I'm a motivational psychologist, Caleb. I specialize in helping my clients reach their full potential."

"You're a shrink?"

She wondered if he'd belittle her job the way her mother did. "Not exactly."

"What *exactly* are we talking about here, Brooke? You are going to continue operating the dude ranch?"

"Good heavens, no. I'm hoping to open a first-class resort where I can work with smaller groups. I don't know the first thing about a dude ranch."

"Then why'd you buy one?" His tone implied she'd lost her mind.

"Because the property suited my needs, or at least it will soon enough."

"What's wrong with it?" He sounded a tad suspicious.

"It's a little too rustic. I'll have to tear down the barns and—"

He shot out of the chair and loomed over her. She

shrank back into her seat, intimidated by the sheer size of him. "Those barns are nailed together with Lander sweat and blood."

The bizarre conversation began to make sense. "I take it you're one of the Landers who bled on my barn?"

"Damned straight. My brothers and I built those barns and we maintained 'em for Charlie while he ran his dude ranch. And we leased his land."

"I understand your concerns, Caleb, and I'm sorry. I won't need barns for the kind of operation I hope to establish. I will need the land."

He paced to the window. Beyond his stiff shoulders she could see the outline of the largest red timber barn blocking the rays of the setting sun. No wonder she'd felt his presence here so strongly. He'd been here all along. He'd probably been in this house, even in this chair. The thought disturbed her. She vaulted out of the chair and circled back to the table and her map—a tangible symbol of her plans for her future. Just seeing the architect's renderings soothed her.

"You've been to one of these *retreats* before?" He asked without turning.

"I've visited several. They're incredibly popular."

"And they're all fancy-pants places?"

Her lips twitched at his description. "The ones I've visited are rather upscale. I've already consulted with a professional about redecorating in a less rustic style."

With his fists clenched by his sides he pivoted and studied her. "Look, sweetheart, we're an hour from anywhere. Dude ranch folks don't mind being in the middle of nowhere, but resort folks expect a few amenities. Those cabins out there are pretty basic."

"And you're an expert?"

"On resorts? Hell, no, but I do know what Charlie's customers expected and what they got. The slicker ones usually complained—a lot—about the distance from the airport, the lack of good restaurants and cable TV. Hell, we don't even have a town of any size in less than an hour's drive. Closest place for supplies is the Farm and Ranch thirty minutes away.''

In a few long strides he stood within touching distance. His scent overwhelmed her senses and his nearness made her skin tingle with the memory of his touch. ''If you want to succeed out here you'll have to have an angle the others don't have.''

His words made her heart sink because she knew he was right. She really hadn't focused on making her retreat unique, only in getting her doors open and her work out there.

He tapped a blunt finger on the cleft of his chin. ''Have you ever considered using the resources you already have and doing your motivational thing on a dude ranch?''

She blinked and made herself focus on his eyes instead of his sensuous lips, but it was difficult when her mind insisted on recalling the amazing things he'd done to her with his mouth in intimate detail. ''I—no.''

''Think of the money you'd save by not ripping out and rebuilding everything.''

He had a point. Several actually. The retreats she'd visited shared the same corporate air. They were almost as anonymous as a chain hotel room, and it was the anonymity that caused her discontent with her public speaking engagements in the first place.

Her snowballing success made it increasingly difficult to connect with people. She couldn't see if her words actually helped when she couldn't make out a single face in the crowd. When she'd decided to redefine her goals, first on the list had been to add more personal contact with her clients.

But was it financially feasible to take a risk on an enterprise she knew nothing about? ''I don't know, Caleb. The developer has already drawn up the plans.''

She gestured to the map on the table. In two long strides he circled the table and bent over the map. He traced the notations the developer had written in with his finger then straightened. ''Give me time to convince you that tearing the place apart isn't the answer.''

Their eyes met and instantly, sexual tension thick enough to walk on filled the room. He cupped her chin. Her breath caught. The rasp of his rough skin made her shiver. Fire flared in his eyes before his gaze dropped to her lips. Her mouth went dry. He stroked his hand down her neck, coming to rest on her shoulder. His fingers tightened, and she recalled his strength, his gentleness, his persistence. He'd brought a part of her to life that she hadn't known existed, a part so needy it frightened her.

Her eyelids grew heavy. She wanted him to kiss her, needed it more than her next breath.

*No, she didn't.* She wouldn't give in to the insanity again. Caleb had made her lose control. She'd fought too long and too hard to gain control of her life to give it up now. It took a colossal effort to smother her body's clamoring demands and push him away.

He dropped his hand and paced back to the window. She heard him muttering under his breath and then he faced her. ''Be ready at seven tomorrow. Dress to ride.''

The front door closed behind him. Through the window she watched him climb on his horse and ride away. The dog trotted behind him. Once he was out of sight she collapsed into the nearest chair and put her head in her hands.

Now she knew why Caleb had come into her life. As the one man who could make her forget who she was and where she was going, his presence was a test of her commitment to her goals.

*Nothing worth having ever comes easy.* Book one, closing sentence.

Caleb slammed the back door. Patrick looked up from his plate. ''I take it the new owner refused to lease to us.''

''She wants to open up some damned California feel-good resort.'' He crossed the kitchen and jabbed the power button on the computer so hard the tower slid across the counter.

''She? You were outbid by a woman? You're kidding me.''

''I wish I were. She says folks pay her for all those little ditties she throws out.'' He tapped his foot impatiently, waiting for the machine to finish its thing so he could get onto the Internet and find out what—*or who*—in the devil he was up against. ''Hell, I thought the way she talked was cute. Didn't know it'd be a curse that would come back and bite me in the—''

''You've met her before?'' Patrick stood behind him, snooping over his shoulder.

Caleb moved the mouse, punched buttons and ignored him. When the search engine appeared he typed in *motivational speakers.* A list appeared and he scrolled down until he saw *Brooke. Brooke Blake.* He hit the hyperlink and her face appeared on the screen. She had her own Web page which only proved she was definitely out of his league. The photo didn't do her justice. Sure, she looked good, but he liked her better with her hair mussed and a glint in her green eyes that warned him she was getting ready to wreak havoc with his libido and his sanity.

''That's her?'' Patrick whistled and put a hand on his shoulder. ''Tell you what, big brother, since you blew it I'll head on over and see if I can convince Ms. Blake to lease us that land.''

The thought of his playboy brother putting the moves on Brooke made him want to hit something. ''No.''

''Marking territory, are you?'' Behind Patrick's surprise was a certain amount of teasing. ''You could always try sweet-talking her into your way of thinking. Scratch that. I forgot it's *you* we're talking about, not *me.*''

''Why don't you shut up so I can read?''

''She's not the hickey-maker, is she?'' A flush warmed

Caleb's cheeks and Patrick hooted. "Oh man, this is going to be good."

Caleb shot his brother an offensive hand gesture. He skimmed down the list of Brooke's impressive credentials and the testimonials of her former clients and his heart sank. Presidents and corporate giants sought her advice. Convincing her to listen to an uneducated cowboy wasn't going to be easy, but he had to find a way. *Had to.* Otherwise, she'd bulldoze his best grazing land.

He'd been desperate when he suggested a motivational dude ranch, and he didn't have a clue what that entailed. He knew the dude ranch business because he'd helped Charlie, but he knew nothing about the motivational mumbo jumbo. Guess it was time to learn. He wasn't stupid enough to go into a fight unarmed.

Returning to the search engine he typed in motivational retreats and started reading. It was his fault they'd lost half of Crooked Creek, but he'd be damned if he'd lose any more.

Patrick patted his back. "Don't take too long figuring out your game plan, bro. Before you know it the calves are going to be hitting the ground and we're going to need those pastures."

Caleb's boots thudded onto her porch promptly at seven. Brooke pulled the door open before he could press the bell. After spending another night dreaming of him she'd awoken tired and frustrated once more. She didn't think she could handle "Happy Trails" this early.

"Let's get something straight. What happened in Tilden won't happen again. I don't sleep with my neighbors."

Embarrassment prickled her skin, but indignation at his blunt statement made her hackles rise. "I don't recall issuing an invitation."

He studied her for several moments as if judging her sincerity then nodded toward the horses he'd left at the foot of the steps. "You ride?"

"No." She'd ridden ponies at camp as a child, but she didn't think a couple of summers twenty-some years ago counted.

"Time to learn. You have a hat?"

She shook her head. He pulled a baseball cap from his back pocket and settled it on her head as if she were a child. "Buy one. Let's go."

"Wait. I have some leftover sausage. Can I give it to your dog?"

"He's not mine. Rico belonged to Charlie and he's barely eaten anything since his master died."

Her heart ached for the mourning dog. She refused to accept defeat so easily. "Can I at least try?"

Caleb shrugged and she raced back to the kitchen to retrieve the sausages. The mutt cocked its head when she knelt and offered the meat, but didn't move from his spot at Caleb's heels.

Brooke tossed the meat on the porch in front of the dog and spoke softly. "Come on, boy."

The dog's nose twitched. He eased forward. After a cautious sniff he gobbled his breakfast.

"Well, I'll be damned."

"I found it in the freezer. I'll cook him some more tomorrow. He looks like he needs it."

She thought she saw approval in Caleb's eyes before he turned and swaggered back toward the horses with the dog at his heels. She wondered if he had any idea how sexy his walk looked from her vantage point. The way he moved was nothing short of spectacular. The man had an athletic grace she rarely saw in anyone other than the professional athletes she occasionally counseled.

Tamping down her improper thoughts, she considered her current situation. The horse looked huge. "Can't we take your truck?"

"Nope. Trail's too narrow where we're going. Come on. Rockette likes ladies. She won't hurt you." He stopped beside the brown horse. When she hesitated he extended his hand. ‘‘Come on, Ms. Blake. Let me show you your property.’’

She hadn’t told him her last name.

The look in his eyes told her refusing wasn’t an option. She moved forward against her better judgment then stopped. ‘‘I’d better lock up.’’

‘‘No need. Nobody ’round here will mess with your stuff.’’

She locked the door anyway. Cautiously she approached the horse. ‘‘Rockette? Why?’’

‘‘Because she darned near kicked my brains out the day I brought her home.’’ She jumped back, but Caleb caught her arm and tugged her forward. ‘‘Don’t worry, she’s settled down since then.’’

He put a piece of something in her hand and guided her palm toward the horse’s mouth. With a delicate nibble the horse took the tidbit. She’d forgotten how downy soft a horse’s muzzle could be. ‘‘Now you’ve made a friend. Let’s get you mounted up.’’

‘‘Why can’t I ride with you?’’ It wasn’t that she wanted to be close to him, but she wasn’t sure she wanted to be alone up there.

His nostrils flared and a spark kindled in his eyes. ‘‘Not good for the horse. Put your foot in the stirrup. Swing your other leg up and over.’’

She tried but her pants were too snug and stiff. ‘‘My jeans are too tight—Aaah.’’

His hand on her bottom boosted her into the saddle. The imprint of his fingers seemed to burn her bottom despite the heavy denim. She grabbed the horn with both hands and surveyed the vast distance to the ground.

Caleb stroked one hand down the length of her leg, positioning it to his liking then he straightened her foot in the stirrup. Circling the horse he repeated the procedure on the opposite side. Beneath her jeans goose bumps rose on her skin.

The man touched her like he had every right to do so.

She'd given him the right that night, but the night was over and she wanted him out of her personal space. She opened her mouth to tell him so, but he spoke before she could find a polite way to state her case.

"You'll need one to steer." He pried one of her hands loose from the saddle horn, laid the reins in her palm, and demonstrated. "Left is this way. Right is the other."

"I don't think I'm ready for this." Her skin tingled from his touch, and it irritated her that he seemed unaffected until she noticed the ridge beneath his fly.

"You're ready." He fed his own horse a tidbit from his shirt pocket then swung into the saddle with a grace she'd never master. He did something and his horse moved toward the field beside the house.

Hers followed. For a while he stayed close, watching her as if assessing her ability to stay on top of her mount. It made her incredibly self-conscious. She fastened a death grip on the saddle horn and hoped she wouldn't disgrace herself by falling off. "Caleb, this tour really isn't necessary."

"I want you to see what you'll be destroying if you plow for a driving range and tennis courts. Later I'll go over Charlie's ledgers with you. You need to know the kind of income you'll be turning away if you close the dude ranch. 'Course, you might make enough off your books that you don't need it."

He'd done his research. She wondered if his behavior would change as a result of who she was. Would he suddenly become a User or a Loser? Experience told her he would.

"Let me guess. You own a computer."

"Yep. If you close down the dude ranch you'll be putting a couple of dozen people out of a job. Not sure they'd measure up to your resort standards and there's not much else around here for them to do."

During the next hour he gave her a guided tour of everything they passed until they rounded an outcropping of trees and stopped. Her horse halted beside his with no bidding from her. With a nod Caleb gestured to a field dotted with deer. Several of the animals lifted their heads then returned to grazing. Rico's ears perked up, but the dog remained quiet beside them.

''Some of the ranchers 'round here lease the hunting rights to their property. Charlie never did.'' He spoke softly, the way he had during their night together. ''The only shooting here was the nature buffs taking pictures. Depending on the time of day you can see just about anything. Deer, turkey, quail, dove, javelina. My brothers and I used to camp in this spot just to see what would turn up. This is where your driving range is slated to go.''

He made his point with a subtlety that surprised her by showing her the animals she'd displace.

He eased his horse back the way they'd come, opening and closing gates as they passed through, and led her down another narrow path. She was becoming accustomed to the rocking motion of the horse and recalling the rudiments of riding when he stopped beside a small pond and dismounted. ''Time to get down and walk or you'll knot up.''

He held up his arms. Reluctantly she slid down into them. After a couple of hours of riding, her legs were as limp as wet noodles and refused to support her. She grasped handfuls of his shirt to keep from collapsing at his feet.

Her mind flashed back in Technicolor detail to that night when she'd willingly knelt before him and he had before her. No matter how she tried to deny it embers smoldered in her belly.

His hands tightened around her waist, supporting her. ''Easy now.''

She looked up at him, wondering if she was the only one unable to forget the passion they'd shared. The spark glittering in his eyes told her he remembered.

''Brooke, stop.''

Shamed by her body's betrayal and by her inability to override her primeval response to his proximity, she licked her dry lips and willed her heart to slow. "Stop what?"

"Looking at me like you want me naked." His voice was deeper, huskier, the way it had been when he'd tangled his fingers in her hair and whispered encouragement for her bold actions.

"And how do you think you're looking at me, Caleb?"

His face and neck muscles tensed. "Like I want to eat you up, but it's not going to happen." He seemed to force his words through clenched teeth.

The intensity in his voice sent another ripple of sensation through her. "It shouldn't."

"It won't." He disengaged her fingers from his shirt and strode toward the pond. His stiff shoulders heaved, and the hands he'd stuffed into his pockets pulled the denim taut across his firm behind.

She really had to stop ogling his butt.

For the first time in her life she had an inkling why some pursued purely physical relationships—two of her former lovers, for example—and she was tempted. So, so, tempted.

# Five

"My brothers and I learned to swim here," Caleb told her without turning away from the water.

Tension strained his muscles, but he had to make an effort to shift them back to safer territory before he did something really stupid like strip those snug jeans off Brooke's long legs and make love to her right here on the ground.

Exhaling slowly, he tried to focus on the reason he'd brought her here. "Irrigating your driving range will drain the pond dry."

She joined him beside the deep green water. He wondered if she realized the color exactly matched her eyes.

"You've lived here a long time?"

"All my life. Same as my father and grandfather." And he'd be the last generation of Landers if her retreat succeeded.

"This used to be your family's property." It wasn't a question, so he didn't reply. "What happened?"

What could he say without revealing what a fool he'd been? He'd bitten the same hook his father and brother Brand had; only his wife hadn't really been pregnant. She'd lied and he'd sucked up her tearful story like a bass eats a worm. He'd believed her right up until the day she'd screamed the truth at him during an argument. She'd even bragged about how easily she'd fooled him.

"My ex-wife wanted her share. I didn't have the cash to buy her off and pay the debts she'd run up. We had to sell part of Crooked Creek to keep her from putting a lien on the entire spread."

"The part you sold became the Double C Dude Ranch?"

"Yep."

"I'm sorry." She sounded sincere.

"Not half as sorry as I am."

He sensed Brooke following him as he walked along the bank. He didn't need to hear her footsteps in the grass, because his body hummed like a divining rod whenever she was near. It had from that first moment in the bar when she'd looked him up and down like he was a T-bone steak, and she couldn't wait to gnaw him clear down to the bone.

She'd taken some coaxing that night, but once he'd put a chink in the dam of her reserve, her passion had raged like Niagara Falls, sweeping them both along until they were gasping and spent. He didn't want to call it the best sex of his life, but… Well, hell, it had been. But that was all it had been. Good sex. And he wouldn't be getting any more of it—not as long as he remembered to think with his brain instead of his—

"Don't we need to tie the horses?"

She was closer than he thought—too close. Close enough that he could touch her silky, responsive skin if he turned and lifted his hand. But he didn't. He'd slipped up earlier and nearly given in to the urge to taste her. He wouldn't again. His marriage and divorce had taught him a valuable lesson—one he didn't need Rockette to kick into his skull. Hooking up with his neighbor had cost him half his land and his best friend—Amanda's brother. His brother-in-law had severed all ties the day Amanda told him her sob story.

"They'll stay put. Besides, Rico's a herd dog. If the horses tried to wander he'd round 'em up.

"I researched your retreat idea. Far as I can tell, there's not another one set on a dude ranch. If you want folks to unwind, you had the right idea buying the Double C, but keeping folks bound up in suits isn't the way to go about it. Jeans and campfires will do the trick."

She chewed her lip. He tried without success to forget the softness of her plump bottom lip and how she'd tasted.

"I see your point, Caleb, but I don't know the first thing about dude ranches. I wouldn't know how or where to find employees."

"Charlie's staff was top-notch. Probably could get most of 'em back with a phone call."

"And who would replace Charlie? Not me. I'm hardly qualified."

That part bothered him a little. Charlie had been trying to hire an assistant for a couple of years, but he hadn't been able to find anybody. Caleb had done what he could to help out.

"Charlie had a trail boss to lead the groups, and Patrick and I included 'em in whatever ranch business we could. It was part of our deal. We leased the land at a reduced rate and in return we let the greenhorns play cowboy. The guests loved it and it worked well for us."

"You know how to run a dude ranch?"

He hesitated, not wanting to admit how much he'd pitched in the last year or two. He had a feeling it would come back to bite him in the butt. "I know a bit."

Brooke's gaze sharpened. "So you could help me find a qualified candidate—if I were to choose the dude ranch route."

All he wanted to do was convince her to lease him her land and to keep the outbuildings intact so that when her retreat failed—and he didn't doubt it would—he'd buy back the Double C and his debt to his family would be cleared. He had a bad feeling about getting roped in. But what choice did he have? "I could try."

"I'll think about it."

As long as she agreed to consider the idea he still had a chance. "Let's head back. We'll go over Charlie's books."

"Why are you so familiar with Charlie's business?"

"I was helping him enter his chicken-scratchings into a computer program. You should have the actual books, but you'll need a CPA and a handwriting analyst to decipher 'em. Charlie Jr. wasn't interested in his dad's *hobby.*" He struggled to keep the bitterness out of his voice, but her curious expression told him he hadn't.

"And you resent that?" Her perceptiveness surprised him.

He wouldn't explain to the woman that she owned the ranch because he'd come up ten grand short when Charlie Jr.'s greed had killed the deal. There was only so much beating a man's pride could take. "I just expected things to turn out differently. Mount up."

She wrinkled her nose. "I'm not sure I can. My legs feel like noodles."

His palms tingled in anticipation of boosting her into the saddle again, but he'd already discovered that handling her curvy behind wasn't a bright idea. The first half hour of the ride out here had been damned painful.

He laced his fingers and bent over. "Step in. I'll lift you."

He hefted her up and then mounted his own horse and led her toward Crooked Creek. He pointed toward the horses grazing in the pasture. "Those are yours."

"I own horses?"

"Twenty of 'em. Didn't you know what you were buying?'' How could she fork out that amount of cash and not account for every nickel? He knew every single item included in the property he'd bid on—right down to the dog trotting beside him.

''I skimmed over the description and took a quick tour of the house and cabins when I first became aware of the auction, but I let my lawyer close the deal. I'm sure he's aware of the details, but I've been touring, closing up my apartment in California and trying to meet a deadline for my next book. I haven't had a chance to study the entire file yet.''

''You got everything but Charlie's clothes and the personal stuff Junior could fit in the back of his car.''

The house came into view. She stopped Rockette. ''That isn't my house.''

''Nope, it's mine. Books are on my computer. Charlie didn't own one. Ignore Patrick if he's around. He chases anything with two legs and estrogen.''

''He's the brother who stayed in ranching?''

''Yep. Supposed to be working in the west pasture with my father.'' He dismounted and helped her do the same, being careful to keep the contact to a minimum, but their knees bumped and tangled anyway. His temperature—among other things—rose.

He took his time unsaddling the horses and turning them loose in the corral. It gave him a chance to get his head on straight before leading Brooke into the kitchen.

The house was quiet and empty when he opened the door. If he'd been a praying man he would've hit his knees and sent up a thank-you. He didn't need Patrick butting in and trying to sweet-talk Brooke.

He pulled a second chair over to the built-in desk. ''Sit. I'll get us some iced tea.''

Brooke's gaze drifted around the room, and he wondered what she'd think of his home. The place was clean enough, but nobody had bothered to paint or spruce up since his ex had redone the entire house more than a decade ago.

Setting two glasses on the desktop, he sat down beside her and clicked opened Charlie's file. A few more clicks and the page he wanted appeared. He focused on the screen, hoping that if he concentrated hard enough he could ignore Brooke's scent. After their night together he knew the taste and texture of each pulse point she anointed with the fragrance.

Whoa. Wrong detour. He cleared his throat and tried to find a comfortable position in the chair. "Here's the bottom line for last year. Gross income. Net profit. Here's the projection for this year. I've already adjusted for the time you've been closed. These figures are based on reopening next month."

He sat back in his chair and let her study the numbers. They impressed the hell out of him, but then he didn't have bestselling books that probably brought in more than the comfortable living Charlie made off his dudes.

Her brows knit as she bent over the pages. She sat back, surprise marking her features. "It was expensive to stay at the Double C."

"Yep. Charlie has—*had*—a long list of return customers, but there's room enough to bring in your motivational folks."

She leaned across him and took control of the mouse. Her elbow brushed his belly and his muscles jumped. He sucked in a deep breath and wished he hadn't. Damn, she smelled good. If he leaned forward just an inch or two he could peel his ball cap off her head and bury his nose in her hair. But he wouldn't.

"This page says there are reservations outstanding."

"Yep. I didn't cancel 'em because I thought I'd be operating the dude ranch for the remainder of the season." Long enough to put a little money in the bank. It wouldn't be a hardship. He kind of liked the greenhorns' enthusiasm for what he considered plain hard work.

"If you're determined to shut down you'll need to notify folks and try to find other dude ranches that'll take 'em. It's short notice. It'll be a problem."

She studied page after page of the file he'd developed for the Double C. Caleb admitted he should have moved to the other side of the room instead of torturing himself. He wanted to touch her so badly his knuckles ached from the tightness of the fists he'd made.

But he wouldn't thread his fingers through her hair or stroke the sensitive spot behind her ear. Just get him through the next hour and he'd steer clear of Brooke Blake until she hightailed it back to California.

He picked up his glass and guzzled the icy liquid. He needed to dump it in his lap.

She pursed her lips and his muscles tensed. Her lips had done some pretty magical things that night. "I'll make you a deal."

He didn't like the sound of that. In his experience women always made lousy deals, and they were rarely satisfied with the result.

"If you'll run the dude ranch for me until I can hire a manager, I'll keep it open for the remainder of the season. It's a trial run, you understand. If it doesn't work out or if I don't like it, I'll close down and next year I'll open my retreat my way."

He bit back the cuss words springing to his lips. She had him over a barrel and knew it. He hoped he had better luck finding a manager than Charlie had. "If I do, will you lease me the land?"

"As long as you're the manager."

"For the entire year or no deal. And you won't tear down any outbuildings during that time." His heart thumped hard while she considered it.

"One year, and I won't make any major changes."

It wasn't a great deal, but it was a start. "I want it in writing."

"Of course." She offered her hand.

Given his dicey willpower, the last thing he wanted to do was touch her, but a handshake sealed a man's word. Or at least it should.

Her grasp was strong, but soft, and it brought back too many forbidden memories of something else she'd wrapped those smooth-palmed hands around.

He released her, probably quicker than was polite and stood. "I'll give you a ride home in the truck."

Brooke frowned at the bottle of liniment Caleb had given her and then at the truck disappearing down her driveway. What was her problem? Each time he slipped her that sideways smile she remembered her disgraceful behavior and her body caught fire like a teenager's.

She made her way to the dude ranch office. Caleb had told her where to find what she needed—right down to which file cabinet drawer contained what. His knowledge was a little disconcerting to say the least. The man knew more about her newly acquired possessions than she did.

She'd avoided coming in here other than to take a quick glance around. The dark paneling on the walls made the room uninviting. Opening the heavy drapes helped dispel some of the gloom. The view from the window took her breath.

After locating the items she needed, she picked up the phone and dialed her accountant and lawyer to tell them the change in plans. She rationalized her decision by reminding them, and herself—that it would be less stressful for her to continue operating the business as it was for the next twelve months. Less stress would enhance her chances of getting pregnant.

She disconnected and sat down in the leather chair behind the desk. Life certainly seemed to be getting complicated since she'd decided to simplify.

Picking up a pen, she pulled a yellow pad of paper forward to jot down a thought. *Your goals must grow and change or they will be defeated by change.*

Less stress wasn't the only reason she'd decided to try things Caleb's way. She had fond memories of giggling girls and campfire confessions from her own preteen years at camp. That innocent stage had ended when she'd discovered how competitive the world and her family could be.

The day she'd overheard her mother discussing her three children with a friend had changed everything. Her mother had described her older brother Robert as bold, bright and determined. Her sister Kathleen had been assigned adjectives like smartest, prettiest and most congenial. When asked to describe her youngest, her mother had sighed and said, "Brooke is my shy underachiever."

There hadn't been one positive word for her to hang onto.

After she'd dried her eyes, Brooke had decided to stop trying so hard to please others and to try to please herself. The first thing she'd done was make a list of what she wanted and then she'd plotted a plan to get it. Of course, she'd never liked stepping on others so she'd tried to motivate her friends to come along on her quest for happiness.

Her career path had been determined at the age of thirteen, and to this day she felt a need to keep pace with her siblings' achievements. Robert and Kathleen had families, homes in the suburbs, and careers to be proud of. She had a career she loved and now a home. All she needed now was a family, and she didn't need a man for that.

Brooke scratched through yet another attempt to write a Help Wanted advertisement. After a frustrating week she hadn't been able to convince any of the Double C's former employees to sign an employment agreement.

Noise outside the office window drew her attention. It wouldn't be Rico. The dog had come for his morning sausage hours ago just as he had every morning since her ride with Caleb. He still wouldn't let her pet him, but he no longer snatched his breakfast and bolted. He'd linger on the porch until she finished her coffee and went back inside. She jotted down a reminder to buy him some regular dog food next time she made it to town. All this sausage couldn't be good for him.

Through the window she spotted three cowboys herding a group of horses into the pen closest to the house. Caleb led the way. Even though she couldn't make out his features from this distance, she could clearly identify him by his confident posture and the battered cowboy hat on his head. And she'd bet those were her horses. Oh joy. The last horseback ride had nearly crippled her. Today was the first day it hadn't hurt to move.

Picking up her new lavender cowboy hat she headed outside. If Caleb was going to be her manager *he* could hire the crew—right after he signed his own contract.

She picked her way through the mud puddles left by the previous night's rain, trying not to ruin her new boots. She was exceedingly pleased that she'd been able to buy boots to match her hat. After all, lavender was her lucky color. The store had even offered a denim jacket and jeans the same shade.

By the time she made it to the fence Caleb had opened the gate and the other men had chased the horses inside. When he'd latched the gate she stepped forward. Caleb's mount snickered, and Brooke recognized it as the horse she'd ridden the other day.

Caleb's head jerked around. He speared her with his dark eyes then let his gaze drift over her in that slow way of his. Her heart rate and hormones responded by fluctuating wildly. Easing forward, she stroked Rockette's neck.

"Good morning."

Caleb dipped his chin and dismounted. His lips were compressed, but the sparkle in his eyes made it look like he might be fighting a smile rather than anger. "Morning. Brought your horses."

The other two riders approached and climbed down.

Both men bore a strong resemblance to Caleb. The older one was a little rougher, the younger one a little more handsome in the conventional sense of the word. She guessed they were Caleb's father and brother. The older man looked at her strangely. The other appeared amused as well.

"Is something wrong?" She looked from the men to Caleb and back.

The younger man stepped forward, removed his hat and offered his hand. His grin was flirtatious, but it didn't affect her the way Caleb's did. "No, ma'am. You must be Brooke. I'm Patrick. This's my dad, Jack."

She shook both men's hands. Caleb stepped forward. "I see you bought yourself a hat."

"Yes. Would you like to come in for something to drink?"

"I—" Patrick started but Caleb cut him off.

"The farrier's due. Patrick needs to head back."

Jack nodded. "I'd better help."

"Nice meeting you, Brooke," Patrick called out as he and his father mounted up. She thought she heard him chuckling as they rode off and left her alone with Caleb.

"Caleb, I'm having trouble rehiring the employees."

"I heard." He unsaddled the horse and turned her loose in the corral with the others.

"I don't understand. You said most of them would want their jobs back, but everyone I interviewed turned me down." She walked toward the house. "I'm hoping you'll help since managing the dude ranch will be your job."

Caleb, carrying the huge saddle, bridle and horse blanket as if they weighed nothing, kept pace beside her. He didn't seem worried about ruining his boots in the puddles. "It's the contract."

"It's a standard employment contract."

"It might be standard in California, but around here folks show up, work and you pay 'em on Friday."

"Without a contract?"

"Yep."

"That's crazy. I insist on an employment agreement—starting with yours."

He stopped at the foot of the stairs with a wary expression on his face. "You expect me to sign a contract?"

"You expect me to sign an agreement leasing you the land?"

"That's different."

"It's exactly the same. I'm promising you something. You're promising me something. You want it in writing. Well, so do I."

"My word is all you need."

"Would you be happy with my promise and nothing on paper?"

His frown bordered on ferocious. "No."

"Charlie did things differently. I'm not Charlie. His business methods were too relaxed for me. I expect you to sign an employment agreement promising to stay on as the dude ranch manager until you hire an acceptable replacement or for one year if you can't find a qualified candidate. In return I'll give you a written guarantee that you can lease the pastures you've previously leased for one year. If you don't sign, I don't sign."

His jaw knotted up. She could see a muscle twitching. For several seconds she thought he'd get on Rockette and ride off behind his family.

He settled Rockette's equipment over the porch railing. "Show me the contract."

"Certainly. It's in the office." She led the way.

Caleb silently ran through his entire list of curses. If he signed he'd be committing himself to spending time with Brooke for a year.

Even though she wore an outfit more fitting to a calendar cowgirl than a dude ranch owner, he still couldn't help noticing the way snug denim cupped her sweet behind or remembering the way his hands had done the same. He didn't think he was strong enough to resist the attraction he felt for her for twelve whole months. He'd have to try harder to ignore the burn in his bloodstream every time she came near, because he couldn't afford to get involved with another neighbor. He'd lost more than he could afford the first time.

He cleaned his boots on the scraper by the door and followed her inside.

"I'll leave you to read over the contract. Can I get you a glass of herbal iced tea or decaf coffee?"

Purple boots. Herbal tea. Decaf. They had absolutely nothing in common, so why did she crank his engine the way no other woman had? Her little ditties? Her determination? The way she wooed an ugly dog? "How about a glass of water?"

"I don't have any bottled water yet. It's obscenely difficult to get it delivered out here."

City women. "From the tap is fine. Your well's been tested. The water's safe to drink."

He read through the contract while she was gone. Unfortunately, he didn't find one single clause objectionable. Picking up a pen, he scratched his signature on the line.

His gut knotted. He'd just agreed to three hundred sixty-five days of sheer torture.

# Six

"Reporting for duty, Boss."

Brooke noted the heavy sarcasm adding an edge to Caleb's words. He hadn't been thrilled to sign the contract yesterday. She opened the door wider and motioned for him to enter.

Rico looked like he wanted to follow, but until the dog had a bath she wasn't letting him inside. Brooke motioned for the dog to stay the way she'd seen Caleb do. He dropped down on the doormat, laying his head on his paws. Slowly she knelt and offered him a doggie treat. After he took it she scratched him behind his ears. He tolerated her touch for all of ten seconds before moving to the porch stairs.

"We have time for an hour's lesson in Dude Ranch 101 before Maria, your chief housekeeper, is due to arrive. Ready?"

She wasn't looking forward to exposing her ignorance. Straightening, she closed the door. "As Yogi Berra once said, *'If you don't know where you're going, you might wind up someplace else.'* I'm committed to continued growth and improvement. Thank you for taking the time to instruct me."

The corner of Caleb's mouth slanted upward. "Love those quotes, Doc."

Darn him. All it took was one crooked grin and a wink to fluster her. She struggled to remember what she'd planned to say. The books and pamphlets stacked neatly on the coffee table reminded her. "I thought we could work in here. The lighting is better."

Lighting had nothing to do with her choice. She couldn't imagine concentrating on business while confined in the small office with Caleb. Being in the same room with him impeded her ability to focus. Before she'd met him she'd been certain she knew exactly who she was and the extent of her limitations. Her life had been organized. One night with him had made her question herself, her values and her abilities.

The more she thought of their night together the more she wondered if her responsiveness had been a fluke, and the more she wanted to test the theory. She suppressed that troublesome thought each time it pushed itself forward, but it kept popping up at the most inopportune times. Like now.

Should she believe in one night of indescribable passion or years of virtual frigidity?

He made his way toward the sofa, but waited for her to sit in the club chair before he sprawled on the cushions with his legs splayed and his—*ahem*—assets displayed. She redirected her gaze and tried to focus on something besides the way the knowledge of what was hidden behind that faded denim warmed her insides.

He gestured to the literature with a nod. "You've been doing your homework."

"I'm trying to learn about dude ranches in general and

my local competition specifically. In return, I'd like for you to read about motivational psychology."

Frowning, he sat up straighter. "You want me to read your books?"

"Yes. I don't normally force my work on anyone, but I plan to teach my methods here. It would help if you were familiar with them. It would be even better if you learned the strategies well enough to reinforce them in your part of the retreat experience."

He crossed his legs and folded his arms, a sure signal that he wasn't going to agree, but then she hadn't expected him to do so without argument. "You want me to spit out your little ditties?"

*Little ditties!* Tamping down her knee-jerk reaction she concentrated on the issue. "Surrounding oneself with positive, supportive people is critical to progress. We need to work as a cohesive unit or..."

"Or what?"

She didn't want to think about the arrows a colleague had aimed at her on a national radio show. He'd put her credibility on the line. He'd pointed out that while she touted having it all she lived alone and wasn't close to her family. "Let's just say that there are those who'd like to see me fail."

He raked a hand over his face. "Why don't you work on getting your guests' heads straight, and I'll stick to keeping 'em from breaking bones?"

"Caleb, for this to work my motivational strategy has to permeate all aspects of our guests' time here. It's a way of life, not just a collection of *little ditties.*"

He digested her reply like a bitter pill. "When do you expect me to squeeze in the pep talk? Between roping and branding lessons, or maybe castrating and deworming?"

He was certainly going to be a challenge, but she'd handled worse. "All I ask is that you learn the principles and keep your mind open. The proper timing will reveal itself."

"Right." He pulled a folded piece of paper from his pocket. "So do you want to know what we have left to do between now and opening day, or should I wait until after Introduction to Cheerleading?"

She sighed and opened her planner to the calendar. It was going be difficult to convert him, but she hadn't given up on anyone yet. In the past her persistence had been rewarded, but Caleb was far outside her realm of experience. Success wasn't guaranteed.

"You can take the books home and read them later. I'll be happy to address your questions as they arise. When are our first guests due to arrive?"

He named the date and her stomach clenched. Her rescheduled appointment at the fertility clinic fell right in the middle of their opening week. She made a note to call the clinic.

Her monthly window of fertility was a narrow twenty-four-hour period, added to which she didn't have all that much time to accomplish her goal of parenthood given her mother's medical history and the reduced fertility of women over thirty-five. However, she would hate to miss the opening week of her new venture. She forced herself to focus on the here and now.

"We'll have to prioritize. Start with the most urgent chores and work your way to the least."

He propped an ankle on his knee, sat back and spread his arms along the back of the sofa. It reminded her of his playful pose in the hotel. He'd sprawled against the headboard, gripped the posts, grinned and growled, "Gonna tie me up this time?"

The memory of how she'd responded sent an illicit tingle through her.

"You'll have the whole house to yourself at night except for when you have singles sleeping in the upstairs rooms. Most folks prefer the cabins. Charlie liked having company. He filled the place to the rafters. He had something going on inside and out, day and night."

"Where will you stay?"

He went still then slowly turned his head until their gazes met. "At home."

"Don't you think you should be here? Isn't there a manager's cabin?"

"Charlie never had a manager, so he never needed a cabin."

"What if something crops up when you're not here?" She should drop it. Having Caleb nearby would ruin any plans she might have for sleep in the near future. He already disrupted her dreams at regular intervals. Why just last night— Heat raced through her bloodstream at the vivid memory of one dream.

"Nothing should happen that your trail boss couldn't handle it. Toby knows his job." He stood and paced to the window. "Brooke, it wouldn't be a good idea for me to stay here."

"You're worried about what people will think? I know it's a small town, but surely—"

"No." His steady gaze locked on hers then drifted over her as thoroughly as he'd caressed her that night. Even from clear across the room the heat in his eyes was unmistakable.

Comprehension dawned. Her mouth went dry. She had to swallow and clear her throat. "You think we'll end up…intimate again."

A muscle ticked in his jaw. "I know we would, but as good as it was between us, I'm not interested."

Humiliated, she rose. Being rejected by the men in her life due to her sexual ineptness seemed to be becoming a habit. "Well, thank you for clearing that up."

When she would have walked away he crossed the room and caught her arm. "Brooke, my ex-wife was a neighbor, my best friend's baby sister. She offered to drive me home from her brother's bachelor party because I'd had too much to drink. I woke up beside her in a hotel room. I didn't remember making love to her, but I was naked, and she swore I'd taken advantage of her. Three weeks later she told me she was pregnant. We ended up in front of a preacher.''

It was rather insulting that he'd compare her to a woman who had to lie to get her man. ''I'm not propositioning you, Caleb.''

''The point is, I became involved with a neighbor, and it cost me and my family half our home-place. I can't afford to lose any more, so I won't risk it.'' He cupped her nape and traced his thumb over her lips. ''Don't think I don't want to. That night was pretty damned incredible. Knowing you were close by and I couldn't touch you would be torture.''

Her heart sprinted. Her breasts and thighs tingled with need. She wet her lips and his eyes traced the path of her tongue. For several heartbeats neither of them moved and then slowly, with a muttered curse, he bent his head. His breath whispered across her lips and her mouth moistened.

The doorbell rang. Caleb jerked away as if yanked from behind. ''That should be Maria. She'll run you through how the house operates, who does what, and what you'll be expected to handle. I'll let her in on my way out.''

Brooke followed Maria around the house taking notes, but her mind was elsewhere. She had a feeling it didn't matter to whom Maria talked or even if they listened as long as the rotund woman had a captive audience.

When she'd excused herself to make a phone call a few minutes ago, the fertility clinic had refused to reschedule her appointment this month. They'd deemed her too far off her expected ovulation date if she tried to come before the first dude ranch guests arrived or after they'd departed. She had to decide which mattered more this month—her possible family or a successful business launch.

She would ovulate again next month, but she'd never have first customers again. However, another postponement left the window open to more potshots from her colleague.

*There is a path around every obstacle if you're willing to search for it.*

Maria clucked with disapproval. "Charlie Jr. should be ashamed of himself, ignoring his father's last wishes like that. Poor Caleb."

Brooke shifted her attention from her dilemma to her housekeeper. "I'm sorry. Poor Caleb?"

"Caleb and Charlie had an agreement and everybody—including that scalawag Junior—knew it."

"What kind of agreement?" From the fierce scowl on Maria's face, Brooke had a feeling she wasn't going to like the answer.

"For years Caleb's been working extra jobs, saving money to buy the Double C back when Charlie retired. But Charlie didn't retire. Old coot died and his low-lying snake of a son got greedy and auctioned the place off. Got more money out of you than what Caleb and his father had agreed on. More money than the place is worth, if you ask me."

Brooke rubbed her abdomen. She needed an antacid. "What kind of agreement did Caleb and Charlie have?"

"A gentleman's agreement. Handshake and a man's word are good enough for most folks around here."

Brooke acknowledged the dig with a wry smile. Caleb had hired the necessary workers, but they had protested loudly before signing their contracts. They hadn't been silent when she'd requested updated job applications or criminal background checks, either. "Caleb didn't consult a lawyer?"

"That I don't know. You'd have to ask him yourself."

"I will." Had she taken what was rightfully Caleb's? And if she had, how could she rectify the situation and still open the retreat?

Doubts crept in. If Caleb and Charlie had had a verbal agreement why would Caleb be helping her now? Would he try to undermine her plans in order to further his own? Her former publicist had certainly had an eye on lining his pockets while handling her business. She was thousands of dollars lighter because of her trusting nature.

"I'm going to the store for groceries. I'll take the ranch truck," Maria said.

The ranch had a truck? She had to carve out enough time to read the thick folder her attorney had given her along with the ranch keys. "Thanks, Maria. If you see Caleb would you send him back to the house?"

The housekeeper took the list Brooke had made and left.

If what Maria said was right and Caleb did have a prior claim on the property, she knew she had to make amends with him, but not right now. Once her new business was a success she'd even the score.

When he finally forced himself to answer Brooke's summons Caleb found her sitting in a rocking chair on the front porch admiring the sunset. She'd kicked off her shoes and her bare feet peeked out from beneath her lemon-colored jeans. Her catalog cowgirl clothes reminded him how unsuited they were, and he needed all the reminders he could get. He'd nearly kissed her earlier, and that was a mistake he didn't want to repeat. Just to make sure he wasn't tempted, he stayed at the bottom of the stairs.

"You wanted to see me?"

"Did you consult a lawyer about your agreement with Charlie?"

He sighed. Maria had been talking. "Yep. He said a verbal agreement wouldn't hold up in court if Junior wanted to fight it. And Junior did. He's married to my ex now, and there's not much about me he likes."

"So why are you helping me when my failure means your success?"

He shrugged. "It's the right thing to do."

She looked skeptical. "How can I trust that you won't sabotage me?"

He inhaled slowly and reined in his temper. She didn't know him well enough to realize she'd insulted the hell out of him. "I gave you my word. I even signed your damned contract."

"In my experience, people don't help their enemies."

The muscles in the back of his neck knotted up. He massaged them. "You're not my enemy, Brooke. None of this mess is your fault. It's mine for not getting Charlie to write down our agreement."

"Still—"

"It's not winning if you have to cheat." He pressed his lips closed. He hadn't meant to yell.

She rose, walked toward him and stopped on the top step. Her eyes, now level with his, narrowed. "You're serious?"

"As a heart attack."

A slow, sexy smile curved her lips, causing his blood cells to herd up and head south. "You really are a white knight, Caleb Lander, whether you want to be or not."

And then she did something he hoped she wouldn't do. She cupped his face, leaned forward and pressed her lips to his. Somehow the hands he lifted to push her away ended up tangled in her silky hair, and instead of drawing back, he opened his mouth over hers and deepened the kiss.

Her surprised gasp turned into that sexy little noise that drove him wild and he lost it. He climbed one step. She descended one. Then they were navel-to-navel, thigh-to-thigh, and chest-to-breast. Her fingers tangled in his shirt, pulling him closer, as if she wanted to absorb him right into her skin. God help him, he wanted to be there.

His hat fell off. Something niggled in the back of his mind, but when she curled one bare foot behind his calf the thought evaporated. He hit his knees, taking her down with him.

The softness of her breasts pushed against his chest as he eased her back against the slatted wood porch floor. When he pressed himself against the apex of her thighs, she made that sexy noise again and raked his back with her nails.

Need escalated with the force and speed of a tornado. It twisted logical thought until he could think of nothing but burying himself deep inside her and satisfying the ache she created.

He brushed his thumb over the beaded tip of her breast. Turning her head to the side, she sucked in a swift breath. Bowing his back, he caught her nipple—shirt and all—in his teeth. She nearly yanked his hair out as she pulled him closer, silently asking for more. And he wanted to give her more. He wanted to free her from the inhibitions that usually caged her, and he knew he could.

But he wasn't prepared.

Harnessing his raging desire was a slow and painful process. He drew away from her inch by protesting inch. His body screamed for the release he knew Brooke could give him, but his common sense—what was left of it—screamed louder.

"Brooke." He peeled her fingers from his hair then unhooked her calves from behind his. "We have to stop."

She stiffened and blinked up at him. Pink spots appeared on her cheeks then she scooted out from under him and clambered to her feet. She looked horrified. "I'm sorry. I don't know what I was thinking. And of course, you were right to stop me. An employer should never—"

"I don't have protection."

She was adorable when she was flustered. He lov—*liked* the way she blushed and her usually direct gaze darted every-which-way but his. "I—oh. Neither do I."

"Getting involved is a bad idea, but risking an unplanned pregnancy is just plain stupid." He looked around for his hat and found Rico guarding it on the bottom step.

"Especially when I plan to get pregnant next month."

He jerked his head up so fast it's a wonder he didn't get whiplash. "Come again?"

Her eyes widened, and she slapped a hand over her mouth. She shook her head. "Nothing."

"You said you plan to get pregnant next month." A sour taste filled his mouth. Acid churned in his stomach. His mother had been a cheater. She'd held on to his father for security and kept a lover for excitement. Eventually she'd dumped them and hadn't come back. "Does your boyfriend know you cheat on him?"

She held up both hands. "I don't have a boyfriend. Please, let's just drop it."

"You nearly ripped my shirt off and you expect me to drop it?"

"It's personal." She looked both indignant and embarrassed.

He snorted. "Yeah, it felt personal to me, too, when you were grinding your hips against mine."

She jabbed a hand through her bangs and huffed out a breath and then started to pace. "I guess you'll find out soon enough. My appointment in Dallas was at a fertility clinic. I missed it because we… Well, you know why I missed it. Anyway, I rescheduled, but now it looks like I'll have to cancel again because the date is during our opening week."

He must have missed something because what she said didn't make a lick of sense. "You're getting inseminated? Like a heifer?"

She winced. "Yes."

"Whose kid is it going to be?"

"Mine. The male component is coming from a donor."

He couldn't believe what he was hearing. "You're going to get knocked up by some guy you've never met?"

She got all stiff and starchy. "I've read his profile. He's a perfect match."

She'd gotten him good. He slapped his thigh and laughed. "You're joking."

Her expression remained serious.

"Right? You *are* joking?" The knot in his gut tightened when she didn't immediately answer.

She sank down on the top step, put her elbows on her knees and propped her chin in her hands. "Caleb, I want a family. I'm thirty-five years old, and I'm tired of waiting for Mr. Right. He's not out there."

"He sure as hell isn't in a test tube." Of all the harebrained ideas.

"I don't expect you to understand. You seem close to your family, but I'm…not. I want someone to come home to at night, someone to hold when things aren't going well or when they are. And my time to accomplish that goal is limited. I guess I'll try again next month."

"You're thirty-five, not fifty-five."

"It takes a woman of my age an average of nine months to get pregnant. My mother was in full-blown menopause at forty and had a hysterectomy by forty-five. I'd like more than one child, and my window of opportunity is closing."

"So why didn't you just try to trick me into it?" Although she'd had her reasons it's what his new sister-in-law had done to his brother Brand. Of course, Brand didn't seem to be complaining.

"Because I want my child to have an ambitious, educated, goal-oriented father."

He rubbed his chest, feeling the sting of her insult. "What makes you think I'm not?"

She offered a sympathetic smile. "Because you're happy staying right here and doing what you've always done. I can't understand why you don't want more."

"Because I have what I need—or I will if I ever get my hands on the Double C."

Her pitying look angered him. "You're missing so much, Caleb."

"What is it with you women? You all think happiness

is out there, but it's not. It's right here.'' He tapped his chest. ''There is no Holy Grail, Brooke.''

''I think you're wrong. As a matter of fact, I make my living teaching people how to tap the greatness within them. Everyone has the potential to achieve their dream.''

Frustration made him want to growl. ''There's nothing wrong with being satisfied with your life.''

''There's an old Chinese proverb that says you shouldn't fear going slowly, only going nowhere.''

''And you think I'm going nowhere because I choose to stay on Crooked Creek?'' Shades of his ex.

''I didn't say that.'' She bit her lip.

But it was obvious she thought it and her assessment burned. He folded his arms and leaned against the porch post. ''I guess I don't have to worry about you tapping into my gene pool.''

''Of course not. You're my employee and I'd never—''

He shoved off the post. ''Sweetheart, I've got news for you. You did back in that hotel room, and you would've right here on your porch if I hadn't stopped.''

Her mouth opened and closed, but no words emerged. The worst thing about the pink flush on her cheeks was that he knew it would extend right down her chest to the tips of her very sensitive breasts.

''Your *employee* is clocking out.'' He pivoted and stomped toward the barn. Nothing like a good ego kicking to end a man's day. It wasn't that he wanted Brooke to have his children. He didn't want any woman having his children.

But he sure as hell didn't like being labeled a reject.

# Seven

Consider Caleb a potential donor? The idea was ludicrous.

So why wasn't she laughing?

In her mind status quo equaled stagnant. The thought of having a day pass without making positive progress toward her goal was unacceptable.

Caleb, on the other hand, held onto status quo for dear life. He wanted the years to pass with no changes to his family's homestead.

She stood between him and his desired outcome. She'd never been the obstacle to someone's success before. It wasn't a comfortable feeling.

She washed down her antacid with a sip of herbal tea and set the rocking chair into motion. Beside her Rico whimpered and cocked his undamaged ear. She reached out a hand and scratched his head. Instead of moving away, the dog laid his muzzle on her knee and watched her with his mismatched eyes. Progress. If only it were so easy to achieve it in the other areas of her personal life.

Her back porch overlooked the corral where Caleb and the group of kids he'd recruited from area ranches put her horses through their paces. He'd said they needed to work the friskiness out before their first guests arrived.

Caleb had a way with kids. He acted like an indulgent uncle—playful for the most part, but firm when necessary. The younger ones seemed to idolize him. The teenage boys respected him, and the teen girls giggled and flirted with him. Obviously his charisma affected women of all ages the same way. She wasn't the only one who experienced an estrogen surge when he was around.

He laughed out loud at one of the boys' shenanigans, and memories washed over her. She'd grown to love Caleb's rumbling laugh during their night together. His lovemaking had alternated between overwhelmingly sensual and playfully erotic. She'd never had fun making love before. The process had always been intense and goal-oriented, but Caleb hadn't let her mistake their one night of passion as anything but a lighthearted romp. And she, who'd *never* indulged in casual sex just for the fun of it, had loved every second.

Her planner lay open on the table beside her waiting for her to get to work, but her concentration was nonexistent. She wrote: *Whenever possible, enjoy your work as much as your play.*

Caleb loved to play. He also loved his work. He'd told her so on their first night together. She saw the proof from her porch. Not that she was spying; she was learning what her new enterprise involved without risking closer contact with the animals and equipment. Or Caleb.

The last thing she needed was an entanglement with a cowboy who lacked the desire to climb the ladder of success, but her thoughts kept straying in his direction regardless of her resolution to keep them elsewhere.

Flipping to the page listing her donor's assets and liabilities, she found herself adding two more columns. Centered above them she wrote *Caleb.* Her sanity must be slipping. Caleb wasn't a potential donor. Making this list was a total waste of time, and she never wasted time. Every possible moment was devoted toward progress.

Her hand moved over Caleb's negative column. *Lacks ambition. Undereducated. Not well traveled. Rough around the edges. My parents wouldn't approve of him. Becoming involved with Caleb would be career suicide. My rival would have a field day if I ended up with an uneducated cowboy.*

*Caleb makes me lose control.*

The entry agitated her so much she switched to the positive column. The list should have been more difficult to fill, but her pen slid quickly across the page. *Sense of humor. Family-oriented. Kind. Considerate. Gentle. Gets along well with others, especially rambunctious children.*

*Makes me feel like a woman.*

She slammed the book closed, wishing she'd limited her list to the items on a real donor sheet: coloring, medical history, height, IQ. Nothing else was relevant to a sperm donor whose only contribution would be impersonal and genetic.

Her donor didn't have dark, coffee-colored eyes deep enough to drown in, nor did he have thick mahogany hair with a slight tendency to curl. Sighing, she wondered if her fluctuating hormones had something to do with her inability to concentrate on work. She'd be ovulating later this week, and she couldn't seem to keep her mind off sex.

Rubbing her temple, she tried to massage away the beginnings of a headache. Rico's excited bark alerted her to Caleb's long stride carrying him across the yard in her direction. Every fiber in her body tensed. While she'd been inattentive another cowboy had taken over with the children.

He climbed the back steps two at a time and loomed over her. "Saddle up."

"Pardon me?"

"You've hidden up here long enough. Your guests are due in a few days, and you don't know the first thing about what goes on beyond that corral. You can't sell the dude ranch experience if you've never done it."

He had a point, but she'd read Charlie's brochures and there wasn't anything in them that she felt a strong urge to experience. She sincerely doubted her corporate motivational clients would want to camp under the stars, catch fish and cook them over an open fire.

"I don't think it's necessary for me to experience baiting a hook firsthand, and for your information, I haven't been hiding. I've been working on my book." Which wasn't exactly true. Her mind had been wandering down forbidden paths. The folder containing her notes remained unopened on the table.

She stood, not wanting to give him the advantage of looking down on her. It placed them face-to-face with not enough space between them, but her chair prevented her from backing up.

She was intensely relieved when he folded his arms, leaned back against the railing and crossed his booted ankles. The move gave her enough room to breathe.

"Never would have taken you for a chicken, city girl."

She drew herself up to her full height. *"Excuse me?"*

The naughty grin on his face caused her stomach to flip flop. "You're afraid something is going to creep into your sleeping bag."

Or some*one*. "I am not."

"Prove it." Pure challenge glinted in his eyes.

Unfortunately she'd always been prone to accepting a challenge. "It's terribly adolescent of you to dare me."

"Is it childish of me to want you to know what folks are forking over their hard-earned cash to see and do?

You said yourself that a stay at the Double C wasn't cheap."

She hated it when he was right. He had valid reasons for her to do something she'd rather avoid, and she didn't need a challenge today of all days. A call from her mother had left her feeling less than her usual confident self. Not even reading her positive thought journal had pulled her out of this funk. And then there were her rampant hormones…

His gaze wandered over her in an assessing manner. "Have you ever been camping?"

"Yes, but like the horseback riding, I don't think a few sessions at summer camp during my adolescence qualifies me for the 'experienced' category."

"Leave the makeup and the city clothes at home and you'll do fine."

She glanced down at the lovely melon-colored denim jeans and matching T-shirt she'd found in the same San Antonio shop where she'd found her lavender outfit. "Why?"

"Light colors show dirt, and you're going to get into plenty of that."

His words didn't increase her enthusiasm, but she acknowledged that a change of scenery might be exactly what she needed. By the time she returned home she might have worked out an alternate approach to achieving her goals. She'd certainly found every possible roadblock to becoming a parent thus far.

"We'll leave in an hour." He turned and left before she could come up with an excuse to bow out. She certainly hoped the thigh exercises she'd been doing would keep her muscles from locking up again. The liniment smelled horrible.

She headed inside to change clothes. Maria met her at the door with the portable phone. "For you. Says he's your lawyer."

"Thanks." She put the phone to her ear. "Phil?"

"Brooke, I have bad news. Our friend has done another radio show."

Had she reached her limit on antacids for the day? "What did he say this time?"

"More of the same. You preach about having it all, but you don't practice it. He's skating close to the line, but he hasn't crossed it yet. Do you want me to take action?"

Only accomplishing her home and family goals would quiet her rival. "If he's not slandering, there's nothing you can do."

"I could always leak to the press about that little cutie his wife doesn't know about." Personally, Phil was a great guy. Professionally, he liked the smell of blood in the water.

"Mud-slinging would only hurt his family. This isn't a political campaign, Phil."

"No, it's your career. I could schedule a rebuttal."

"Attack the issue, not the person. And right now he has me on the issues."

"Isn't that a line from your last book?"

"Yes. I have everything under control. In time I'll prove him wrong."

"Hopefully before your next book is released. I hate to see what this will do to your sales numbers."

So did she. She found herself repeating Caleb's words. "It's not winning if you have to cheat."

Caleb stood behind Brooke as she lowered the rifle. He shouldn't have been surprised that she handled the gun competently, but he was. She'd hit two of the ten skeets he'd tossed. "Not bad for a city girl."

"The safety course didn't teach us to hit moving targets." She cleared the chamber and efficiently put the weapon back in its case. Smooth, confident, capable. It was difficult to dislike someone with those traits. "What's next?"

"Most of your guests will want an evening ride as well

as a morning one, but we'll skip that. When we bring 'em this far away from the homestead, we'll truck the horses and people out like we did today."

"We should have brought Rico."

"He gets carsick. Patrick will make sure he eats." The setting sun silhouetted her curves, and he reminded himself that she was his boss now. He had no business looking at her and remembering how she looked naked.

He cleared his throat. "The crew sets up camp while folks are skeet shooting and cleaning their catch. You'll be sorry you threw that bass back. He would've been tasty."

She grimaced and walked toward the campsite. "Now that I've met him, I don't want to eat him."

"Sissy." He couldn't help grinning.

Brooke was a strange combination; tough as nails one minute then squeamish the next, but she'd cowboyed up and tried everything he'd thrown at her this afternoon. And he was ashamed to say he'd thrown quite a bit. He had to admire her grit. Now all he had to do was get her to loosen up. He'd never met anybody so intense about every single thing. No wonder she always popped antacids.

When he'd spotted her moping on the porch he'd known he had to do something. Introducing her to the reality of ranch life was as good a way as any to get a feel for how long she'd last outside the city limits. As long as he reminded himself that sooner or later she'd leave he wouldn't miss her…much. Besides, her leaving would be a good thing. He'd get his land back.

She studied the area he'd cleared for their sleeping bags then surveyed the falling darkness closing in on them. "I wish you'd let me bring a tent."

"Can't see stars through canvas." He'd suspected from the get-go that she wouldn't like sleeping in the open, but she needed to try it since most of her guests would elect to rough it once or twice during their stay. The dude ranch offered tents to the persnickety guests, but he wasn't willing to risk the intimacy of sharing a tent with Brooke.

Judging by the smell, the potatoes he'd wrapped in foil and set inside the fire ring were almost ready. He crouched by the blaze and positioned the metal grate over the rocks. "You never met the steer. Think you can eat the steak?"

"Funny." She knelt beside him, warming her hands by the flame.

The temperature had dropped, giving the September air a bite. As she scrubbed her hands together the firelight reflected off the gold necklace hanging in the shadow between her breasts.

The steaks sizzled when he laid them over the flame. The aroma reminded him he'd forfeited lunch to prepare for this outing. "You said you camped as a kid."

"It was only one week each summer from the time I turned ten to the summer of my twelfth birthday."

"Why'd you stop? Didn't like it?"

"I loved it, most of it anyway, but it was time for me to set the course for my future. I started working." There was an edge to her voice he didn't understand.

"What kinds of jobs?"

"I was a page in the House of Representatives, and a girl Friday for a judge."

"Serious stuff." He should have known she wouldn't choose something as normal as baby-sitting or mowing grass like regular folks. "You were an ambitious kid."

"I had to be to compete with my superachieving older siblings. Robert is a Wall Street whiz kid. Kathleen is a fund-raising maven. They are the pride and joy of our parents."

"You're the odd man out?"

She shrugged. "It seems that way sometimes. My work isn't exactly vital."

"Would you trade your job for either of theirs?"

She didn't hesitate. "Good heavens, no. Both work sixty-hour weeks and rarely see their families. They also work with numbers instead of people. I couldn't stand that."

"And yet you consider them more successful than yourself."

She frowned and stared into the flames. "I guess I do."

"If it's not the job you want, then you shouldn't envy somebody else for having it. My brother Brand had a job most men would dream about. He was a rodeo champ. He raked in the money and always had pretty women chasing him. As good as that sounds, it wasn't for me, because he was almost never home and this is where I want to be."

A few moments passed with nothing but the crackle of the fire and the hiss of the steak juices hitting the logs to interrupt the silence of the night. Brooke seemed lost in thought and then she looked up.

"What happens during dinner? The pamphlet said something about Western folklore."

He'd given her something to chew on, so he let her change the subject. "While the cooking's going on your trail boss will tell some cowboy tales."

"Do you know any?"

He shook his head. "Toby's your man. I'm about as entertaining as a bellyache. Can't seem to get the punch-line right."

Brooke's expression turned serious. "You told me you married your wife because she was expecting, and yet you don't have a child. What happened? Did you lose custody?"

He nearly dropped the steak as he turned it. If he didn't tell her somebody else would. "Amanda lied. There wasn't any baby. We hadn't even slept together. She set me up. We were married before I figured it out."

"Oh, Caleb, I'm sorry."

"Not half as sorry as I am. Her brother was my best friend—until she told him I'd taken advantage of her. That killed our friendship. I don't miss Amanda, but I sure miss

Whitt. For twenty-two years he was like another brother to me.''

''What did he say when you told him the truth?''

''Didn't. Wasn't much point. By then I had slept with her. Hell, she was my wife. I just figured we'd make the best of it.'' He turned the potatoes and stirred the beans. ''If we're going to ask difficult questions here, you're going to have to tell me why you've written off finding Mr. Right.''

She looked like she'd prefer taking a nature call in the dark to answering his question. ''I've been involved not once or twice, but three times before and each time it's ended disastrously.''

He whistled. ''Why'd you dump 'em?''

He didn't doubt Brooke had been the one to end the relationships. No man in his right mind would let her go. He was beginning to doubt his own sanity.

''My first lover was my college professor. He helped me get my first book published, and then he slept with my roommate. End of relationship. My second was my publicist. I found out he loved my money more than he loved me, but not until after we were engaged and we shared joint bank accounts. End of relationship number two.''

She stood and paced laps around the fire until he thought he'd get dizzy. ''I wanted a family. As I told you before, my time to conceive a child is limited by my medical history.

''I'd chosen badly twice, so I decided to trust in my father's choice. My last involvement was with Dad's protégé. Unfortunately William just wanted to score points with his mentor—even if that meant being with me. The day I found him with his gay lover is the day I told him goodbye.''

Finally she stopped directly across the fire from him. ''I guess you could say I don't have great taste in men.''

He winced. ''Hey.''

She grimaced and shrugged. ''Present company not excluded. You're so wrong for me, Caleb...but I want you anyway.''

He dropped his steak into the fire and didn't care. All he could do was stare at Brooke. ''Say what?''

She bit her lip and tugged the hair at her brow until it stood up like a rooster's comb. ''It's crazy, but I keep... That night...'' Taking a deep breath, she started over. ''I've never enjoyed making love the way I did with you. I had even convinced myself that my previous lovers turned to others because I was frigid. But I wasn't with you. And I can't forget it. I keep reliving that night and wondering if my reaction was a fluke.''

He couldn't believe what he was hearing. Anger toward the jerks in her past nearly consumed him. He'd never met a more sincere woman, but right now he couldn't help wishing she'd be a little less straightforward with her feelings.

''It wasn't a fluke, Brooke. You're so damned responsive I—'' The gnawing hunger pains in his stomach headed south, stirring up a more ferocious appetite. Fisting his hands, he walked toward the darkness.

The ache in his groin throbbed for attention. Brooke's attention. But not only was she his employer, she owned the land he one day planned to buy. Dammit, call him all kinds of fool, but he didn't want her to think he was just another jerk in the long line of jerks who'd used her.

He called over his shoulder, ''Finish your dinner and bed down. I'm going to see to the horses.'' The horses were fine. He'd done what needed doing earlier, but he needed space and time to rein in his hormones.

''Caleb.'' She touched his arm and every muscle in his body clenched. ''Make me believe it wasn't a fluke. Make me believe that I'm not some flawed excuse for womanhood.''

The uncertainty in her voice nearly did him in, but he

didn't turn. If he did his will to resist her would be toast. "You're my boss."

"And I want you to know that your answer—whether affirmative or negative—will in no way affect your position."

He couldn't move, couldn't speak. He wanted her, and he knew damned well he shouldn't accept her offer.

She removed her hand. "It's okay. I know I'm demanding and slow to arouse. I—"

Her willingness to accept defeat angered him, and it seemed out of character given her Can Do stance in her books. Caleb jerked around to face her. The doubts on her face twisted his insides. At the risk of pulverizing his good intentions, he tipped up her chin with his finger and waited until she met his gaze.

"You know exactly what turns you on, and you're not afraid to ask for it. Don't apologize. It's as sexy as hell. But Brooke—"

Her eyes warmed with his words. She cupped her hand over his and carried his fingers to her lips. "I hate the word 'but.' Negative thoughts yield negative actions."

Another little ditty. They were just words. Why did he find them sexy? "Right. But this is not a good idea."

Her tongue slipped between her lips to taste the pad of his finger in a long, slick swipe. His knees nearly buckled.

"It wasn't a good idea the last time, either, but it was wonderful. You have to know what you want and not be afraid to go after it, Caleb. I want you. I'm not asking for anything long-term. I just want to know if that night was an aberration."

He couldn't pull enough air into his lungs. When he tried, the stench from the burning steaks made him cough. He'd wanted her to loosen up, but he hadn't bargained on this.

Freeing his hands, he clasped her waist and tried to put an inch or two between them before she felt the ridge in his jeans.

''Dinner,'' he protested.

She must have sensed his indecision because she smiled that slow, sexy smile that caused his gut to knot up. ''I'm not hungry for steak.''

The husky tone of her voice sent his good intentions the way of his dinner. Up in smoke. She was offering no-strings-attached pleasure. No expectations of wedding bells. It bothered him more than a little that she wanted a baby, but she already had her stud lined up, so he was in the clear as long as he was careful.

''Are we talking tonight, a week, the entire year?''

''As long as it feels good.''

''Are we going to have to put this in writing?''

Her womanly laugh drove his blood pressure through the roof. ''I don't think so.''

With a groan, he surrendered to the need burning in his blood. Their mouths smashed together with the force of a car wreck. He tightened his hands around her waist and drew back to check for damage.

''Whoa, Brooke. Easy now.''

She responded by locking her hands behind his head and recapturing his mouth. Desperation flavored her kiss, infusing it with a frantic need that escalated his own.

With a quick jerk she unsnapped the entire placket of his shirt then pressed her lips to his chest and laved him with her tongue. His skin ignited. He tangled his fingers in her hair and angled her head to kiss her again.

Beneath her adventurous hands his belt buckle gave way. She pulled his shirttail free, and skated her soft hands across his back then down to cup his buttocks. Given his state of near detonation, she was moving too fast. He scooped her into his arms, laid her on the sleeping bag and knelt over her.

Capturing her arms, he pinned them beside her head and arched out of reach of her voracious mouth. ''You want to tell me what's really going on here?''

She bit her lip and closed her eyes tightly. ''You should

never end a day on a negative note. It's been a really bad day. I need something good to happen.''

He *should* be insulted, but he was having a really hard time being anything but turned on. ''I'm a reward for toughing it out, huh?''

''Yes. Does that make me a bad person?'' Her eyes beseeched him and his heart softened.

''No, it makes you an honest one, but, sweetheart, I have to warn you that I don't do *good.*'' He waggled his brows and winked. ''I specialize in five-star service, ma'am.''

A smile curved her damp lips. ''I think I'll have to judge that for myself.'' A challenge. Damn, he lov—*liked* her dares.

He transferred her wrists to one hand and slipped a finger beneath her waistband, running it left and right, dipping a little lower with each pass. When he encountered the hem of her T-shirt he hooked it and tugged upward to reveal a sliver of pale skin. He bent to nibble the spot and heard her gasp.

''You see at Double C it's the special touches that enhance the dude ranch experience.'' He eased her shirt up farther, tasting her navel, her ribs, savoring the softness of her skin.

When he uncovered her breasts, his throat closed up. Her peach bra was so sheer she might as well be naked. Under his gaze her rosy nipples tightened and puckered. His hand shook, but with a flick of his fingers, he managed to get the front clasp of her bra to open. He nuzzled the fabric aside and sampled the underside of each silky globe with his tongue and teeth.

''I've never made love outside before.'' She squirmed beneath him and struggled to free her hands, but he didn't release her. He was too near the end of his tether to let her touch him. He knew how dangerous her hands could be.

''I'm more than willing to do my part to further your

education.'' He tugged up her T-shirt until it tangled around her wrists. ''Don't move.''

Her jeans were new and the denim was stiff and uncooperative. Her gyrations didn't help. By the time he'd peeled her pants and panties down to her boots, he was breathing like he'd just wrestled a steer. Of course, Brooke's skin was much more supple than a bovine's. He traced a hand over her satiny curves, down her legs, and back up to the tangle of golden curls. She was already wet and swollen. He made quick work of ridding her of her boots and socks.

She started to reach for him, but he shook his head. ''Stay put.''

He shucked his own clothing in record time then dug into the saddlebag for the protection he'd bought during his hasty trip to the local ranch supply store. He didn't hesitate to rip open a package and roll it on.

''You planned for us to make love tonight?'' Her breathless voice combined with the sight of her bare skin in the moonlight and the flickering firelight erased what little patience he had left.

''No. It's not something I'm proud of, but I can't be near you without wanting to be inside you. I thought I'd better be prepared—just in case.''

She tossed off the shirt restraining her wrists and held out her arms. ''Then you're awfully far away, cowboy.''

He fell to his knees between her legs. Cupping her feet in his hands, he kissed the inside of her ankles, her calves, her knees. ''Here at the Double C we always make sure the stirrups are adjusted to the rider.''

He hooked her ankles behind his back and leaned down to capture a rosy-tipped breast in his mouth. The warmth of her satiny folds cradled him, invited him. It took every ounce of his control to rein in his desire and not plunge inside her, but before he gave in to the need burning him alive he was going to erase all her doubts about her abilities as a lover.

She captured his head, holding him close while he suckled and laved her. She was so sensitive and he wanted her to unwind all over him. He paid close attention to the flush warming her skin beneath his lips and to the increased tempo of her breathing as he stroked her slick heat. She twisted beneath him, arching and making that sexy sound that drove him wild. He nearly lost it.

The soft skin of her belly drew him like a moth to a flame. He nibbled his way across her quivering abdomen to the curls between her legs. The heady scent of her arousal sent a shudder through him and he fought for control. His hunger for her threatened to consume him the way the campfire had consumed their dinner.

The taste of her on his tongue only increased the ache in his belly, but he pushed her over the edge again and again until she lay limp beneath him. Pressing a kiss on the inside of her thigh, he asked, "Still think your response is a fluke?"

She feigned a puzzled expression, but he didn't miss the amused sparkle in her eyes. "I'm not sure yet."

He choked out a laugh and hugged her close. This rarely seen playful side of her was an incredible turn on. "Witch. I guess I'll just have to keep trying to hammer home my point."

"Please do."

Unable to resist any longer he thrust deep. She welcomed him inside. Fire raced through his veins, and he couldn't ride fast enough or stroke deep enough to escape the need burning him alive.

Her nails scored his back, his buttocks, intensifying his pleasure tenfold. She bit his shoulder hard enough to leave a mark just before she called his name in that breathless whimper that told him he'd done his part to turn her inhibitions loose. Deep inside she contracted around him, and he couldn't hold back any longer. Shudders racked through him as his passion pulsed free.

Spent, he held her in his arms and rolled to her side.

His heart raced. His breath burned in his lungs as if he'd run a mile. He couldn't have strung a sentence together if his life depended on it. His muscles and brain had melted. Making love to Brooke was something he could get used to, and her no-strings-attached rule seemed like a gift from heaven.

So why did it leave him wanting more?

Lethargic and satisfied, Brooke curled against Caleb, twining his chest hair around one painted fingernail. There wasn't anything wrong with her sexually. Caleb had given her an incredible gift by easing a little of the blame she'd shouldered for the failure of her relationships, but then Caleb was like that. He always seemed to be looking out for others.

A decision based upon her knowledge of Caleb's generosity and her earlier journal notes clicked into place like the cylinders of a lock when the right key is turned.

Adrenaline raced through her system. Caleb could open the door to the one goal that had escaped her thus far.

"Caleb?"

"Mmm?" He sounded half-asleep.

She took a deep breath. "Would you father my baby?"

# Eight

Caleb's muscles knotted and his expression hardened.

Brooke sighed with disappointment. She hadn't expected him to welcome her idea with open arms, but she had hoped he'd at least consider her offer. She pressed her fingers over his lips. "Hear me out. Please."

He flinched away from her touch and scowled. Pulling from her arms, he rolled to his feet and snatched up his jeans.

The chill of the night and Caleb's silent rebuff enveloped her. Shivering from a combination of the cold and nerves, she wrapped the edges of the sleeping bag around herself. "Caleb—"

"No the hell way." He continued yanking on his clothes.

"I have something you want."

His dark gaze speared her then slid over her like a rough caress. "As good as the sex is between us, it's not worth the price you're asking."

She ignored the sting of rejection and shook her head. ‘‘I meant land. I’ll give you the land if you’ll give me a child.’’

He froze with one boot half on. His eyes narrowed. ‘‘Say again?’’

‘‘I’d need to keep enough acreage to run my retreat, but I’ll sign over the pastures you’ve leased in return for your…contribution.’’

‘‘What happened to your perfect donor?’’ Sarcasm hardened his voice.

Yes, what had happened to him? She’d begun to wonder if traits like patience, generosity and consideration were genetic. They were certainly traits she wanted her child to have, but they weren’t found anywhere on a donor fact sheet. ‘‘He’s just facts and figures on a piece of paper. It could be lies for all I know. You, on the other hand, are a living, breathing, healthy specimen.’’

‘‘Specimen,’’ he muttered under his breath and hauled on his other boot with terse, angry moves. ‘‘No.’’

This wasn’t going well, but she’d never been one to accept defeat easily. Her timing and delivery were wrong, that’s all. ‘‘Why not?’’

He glowered at her from across the fire. ‘‘Because I’m not some damned stud for hire. Forget it.’’

‘‘Caleb, be reasonable. You need the land.’’

‘‘I. Am. Not. For. Sale.’’ He enunciated each word separately and with enough force to pound it through her head. ‘‘Get dressed. We’re going back.’’

He smothered the fire and the charred remains of their dinner and stalked off toward the horses.

Reluctantly she pulled on her clothes. She’d offended him and that hadn’t been her intention. He ought to be flattered that she considered him worthy of fathering her baby. Okay, so he hadn’t gone to college, but she’d discovered over the last week that he was an intelligent man. And he wasn’t blond, but dear heavens, the man would make beautiful babies. Her heart lurched as she pictured a chubby-cheeked, dark-haired, dark-eyed child.

Caleb's lack of ambition would always be an issue, but she wouldn't let that worry her. She could instill the hunger for self-improvement in her child. After all, that was her vocation, and she excelled at it.

She rolled the sleeping bags and stowed them in the bed of the truck then gathered the other items scattered around the campsite while he loaded the horses into the trailer. When she finished she climbed into the truck cab and waited until he joined her.

"Caleb—"

"Don't. I'm about as angry as I've ever been in my life, and I don't have one polite thing to say." He cranked the engine with such a savage twist it's a wonder the key didn't break off in the ignition.

The ride back to the ranch was bumpy, silent and tense. She had the strange feeling that she'd disappointed him somehow. The headlights caught scattering deer and other animals she didn't recognize. In other circumstances she would have asked him to slow down to let her look, and she would have asked him to tell her about the animals. He was incredibly knowledgeable about the land and its inhabitants.

Caleb stopped the truck at the end of her front walk. His muscles bunched beneath the hand she laid on his arm.

"Please think about my offer."

"Nothing to think about." In the dim lights from the dash she could barely make out his tense features, but the hostility radiating from him was unmistakable. He faced her with a jerk. "What kind of sonofabitch do you think I am that I'd father a kid then abandon it?"

"It wouldn't be like that."

"You're proposing?" His sarcasm stung. She didn't need to see his sensual lips to know they'd be twisted with scorn.

"Of course not, but artificial insemination is perfectly acceptable these days. Many single, professional women are making the same choice."

"Not with me." He twisted in his seat, bracing his arm on the steering wheel and the other on the back of the seat. His fists clenched. "My mom walked out on us when my baby brother was two. I know how tough it is to be part of a broken family. Do you?"

Brooke bit her lip. "I'm sorry. I didn't know about your mother. My parents haven't always been supportive, but they have always been there. But I've thought this out, Caleb. I know I could be a good mother."

He silently faced forward and reached for the gearshift, effectively ending the conversation.

"Good night." With a sigh, Brooke let herself out of his truck and made her way up the walk. She'd give him time to reconsider. Surely he'd see that her offer made sense. In the meantime, she'd try to amass more arguments in her favor. Caleb seemed like the type of man who would listen to reason.

Patrick met Caleb as soon as he pulled into the yard. "I've been looking all over for you."

Alarm tingled through him, erasing the disappointment weighing him down. Brooke was just like every other woman in his life. She wanted something from him. Once she got it she'd move on. "What's wrong?"

Patrick headed for the rear of the trailer, calling over his shoulder. "Brand called a couple of hours ago. He and Toni are at the hospital. The babies are coming."

Caleb's muscles locked at the mention of babies.

Patrick smacked him on the arm. "Come on. Get the lead out. Dad's already left."

"It's not like you're going into the delivery room, so what's your hurry?" He backed Rockette out of the trailer and led her to her stall while Patrick dealt with the other mare.

"Brand doesn't ask for much. He wants us there. I plan to be there. I think he's scared."

Caleb snorted. "Give me a break. Our little brother rode bulls for a living. He's not going to be scared of a baby."

"I think he's worried about Toni. She's had it rough these last couple of weeks."

His brother had certainly fallen completely for the woman who'd roped him into a shotgun wedding by deliberately getting knocked up.

Caleb's stomach muscles tightened. If Brooke had her way, she'd be doing the same thing to him. And he didn't need a fortune-teller to predict what would come next: tears, recriminations, a broke cowboy.

He'd lived that life already and wasn't eager to repeat his mistakes.

After unhitching the horse trailer, he climbed back into the truck. Patrick vaulted into the seat beside him. "You took your lady out for a moonlight ride and you came back before midnight. How'd you screw it up?"

"I didn't." If Patrick heard the entire story, he'd freak out. Nobody ran faster from responsibility than his younger brother. But some things a man just shouldn't discuss.

"You losing your touch?"

He hit the steering wheel with his fist. "Do you want to walk?"

"She kicked you out?" Laughter laced his voice.

"None of your damned business." He wondered how long it would take for Brooke to find someone who was willing to grant her request and why in the hell he cared. He didn't, dammit.

"So how long do you think she'll last?"

He feigned ignorance. "Who?"

"Brooke, you turkey. How long before her retreat fails or she gets tired of being stuck in the middle of nowhere?"

What concerned him more was how long it would be before she became a mother and decided to raise her kid somewhere besides backbreaking cattle country.

"I don't know." She had more grit than he'd expected, and he sure as hell couldn't figure out how her mind worked. Her proposition had come out of nowhere.

"Well, God help us if she gets married and has kids before she hightails it back to California. You might never get your hands on the Double C."

Acid churned in his stomach. He'd been done out by one heir. If Brooke went through with her insemination plans next month, would he be done out again? And the thought of her hooking up with another one of her loser boyfriends made him want to put his fist through something.

Caleb knocked on the hospital room door and shoved it open when Brand called, "Come in."

He stopped in his tracks. Brand stood beside the bed cradling a tiny, blanket-wrapped bundle in his arms. Toni, looking tired but happy in the bed, held another. Both babies had red faces and little pink and blue striped hats on their heads. It wasn't the babies that stopped him. It was the emotion on his brother's face that put a knot in Caleb's throat and made him uncomfortable. Brand looked like somebody had just handed him the world.

He hoped nobody ever snatched it back. There were some things a big brother just couldn't fix. Like a broken heart.

"Move." Patrick shoved him out of the doorway.

Caleb cleared his throat. "Everybody all right?"

Brand grinned. "Couldn't be better. Short labor, healthy babies, beautiful wife." He winked at Toni. "Ya'll wash up and put on one of those gowns. It keeps the germs under control."

Patrick beat him to the sink. They each donned a hospital gown over their shirts and jeans. The baby Brand held squirmed inside its blanket cocoon and made squeaky noises.

"Miranda is hungry," Brand said. "Has Marissa finished?"

Toni shifted the blanket draped over her shoulder. Caleb figured out exactly what was going on under there. Heat crept up his neck and face. Even though he couldn't really see anything he turned his head. It seemed pretty darned personal to be in here when the baby was doing *that.* Brand and Toni exchanged babies. Toni reached for the opening in her gown, and Caleb wanted to bolt right back out the door.

Patrick stepped toward Brand. "Lemme see the little critter."

Brand held the baby tucked in his arm like a football. "This is Marissa. She's the oldest by ten minutes. Here, wanna hold her?"

Patrick shrunk back. "Caleb said he wanted dibbs."

With everybody looking at him Caleb couldn't call his brother a liar. He didn't have much choice but to take the baby Brand offered.

He hadn't held a baby since his youngest brother Cort had been born almost twenty-three years ago. This one didn't weigh much and he was terrified he'd drop her. Brand tugged off the little tike's hat and fluffed her fuzzy blond hair then put the hat back on. "They're both gonna look like their momma. Little blond angels. Just what I asked for."

Caleb sank into the chair beside the bed because his knees were shaky. Blanket and all, Marissa wasn't as long as his forearm. One of her tiny hands flailed. She blinked up at him with blue eyes. Instinctively he offered her a finger, and she grasped it, capturing him. His throat burned. His chest felt tight.

Brooke wanted a baby. His baby. And since he'd refused her request, whose baby would it be? He glanced at the bed. Would Brooke take her baby to her breast?

Would she wear the same happily dazed expression his sister-in-law wore? Would she stare at him with the love that Toni openly showed Brand?

Whoa. Put the brakes on that thought. There was no love between him and Brooke. They barely knew each other except in the Biblical sense.

She'd give him the land if he'd father her child. His chance to reestablish Crooked Creek was within his grasp. Was he willing to pay the price she asked? Hell no, he couldn't father a child and walk away from it, but he owed it to his family to regain the land his mistake had cost them.

Could he find a way to make Brooke's crazy idea work to his advantage? Could he find a way to keep her from taking their child and heading back to California?

He looked away from the trusting blue eyes to his proud-enough-to-bust brother. "What kind of deal did you and Toni make?"

Brand looked surprised. "What?"

"When you found out Toni was pregnant what kind of deal did you make to keep her from running off with your kid—kids?"

Brand and Toni exchanged a glance. Even though they'd never discussed their relationship with him, Caleb knew they'd had some tense times before they'd worked things out. Given what he knew about twins coming early, it didn't take a mathematician to count back and know Toni had either been pregnant before their rushed wedding or had become so on their honeymoon. He tended to believe the former since he'd heard rumors about Toni and Brand and Vegas from Brand's rodeo buddies.

Finally Toni offered, "We had a prenuptial agreement drawn up. I provided the land and Brand provided the money."

"Anything else?"

After a nod from Toni, Brand added, "We had a clause that said if one of us leaves the ranch, the other would get full custody of the kids. Of course, that's not going to happen now, but we didn't know that then.''

''Right. Dad's still here?''

Brand nodded. ''He's looking for the vending machines.''

''Then he can give Patrick a ride home. I have to go.'' He stood, passed the baby off to a startled Patrick, peeled off the protective gown and headed for the door.

''Hold it.'' Brand caught him out in the hall, stopping him with a hand on the shoulder. ''What's going on?''

He debated how much he should share with his brother. Brand had inside knowledge on the workings of a woman's mind. ''I found a way to get the other half of the ranch back.''

''Patrick says some chick outbid you. If you need money—''

''It's not my money she wants.'' He held his brother's gaze and tipped his head toward Toni's door. Comprehension dawned in Brand's eyes. He confirmed it. ''She wants me to father her baby.''

Brand swore. ''Caleb, Toni is the best thing to ever happen to me, but it could have easily gone the other way. Think hard before you make that kind of decision.''

''Right.'' He headed for the elevator.

''And get yourself a good lawyer,'' Brand called after him.

Persistent hammering woke Brooke from a deep sleep. She squinted at the clock and groaned. She'd tossed and turned for hours after Caleb had dropped her off, and had only fallen asleep a short while ago.

Shoving her hair out of her eyes, she shrugged into her robe and stumbled toward the front door. Who would be knocking at this obscene hour? She cursed the lack of a peephole and reminded herself to have one installed when she had an alarm system wired.

''Who is it?''

''Caleb.'' Her heart skipped a beat. She couldn't catch her breath. ''Open up, Brooke.''

She flipped on the porch light. Clutching her robe tighter, she eased open the door. He still wore the clothes he'd been wearing when he dropped her off, and he looked as rough as she felt. His hat was missing and his hair looked like he'd been running his fingers through it. As if to prove her point, he did just that.

''Come in.''

He brushed past her, heading straight for his favorite spot in front of the large window. Caleb didn't say a word. He just stared at her through narrowed, assessing eyes.

Her nerves were shot. She was too tired for a staring match. Why was he here? ''Caleb, it's four-thirty in the morning.''

''I'll do it.''

She snatched a quick breath and pressed a hand over her jolted heart. He couldn't mean what she thought.

''But only if we spell out every detail in writing beforehand. And I want custody of the kid if you leave the Double C.''

She scrambled to make her sleep deprived brain make sense of what he said. ''No. I mean, yes, to having a legal document state the particulars, but no, I won't give you custody. Why would I go to so much trouble to have a child only to give it away?''

''You're planning to leave?''

''No, but no one can predict the future, Caleb.''

''I want joint custody then.''

She needed to be writing this down. Where was her planner? She glanced around then remembered she'd left it on the bedside table. The last entry had been more reasons why Caleb was and *wasn't* good father material. Could she actually be standing here considering sharing her child with him? ''Is that negotiable?''

''No.'' His locked jaw warned her it would be a waste of time to argue.

"Hold on a second." She raced to her room, found her planner and raced back to the den. She sat on the couch and quickly flipped to a clean sheet before he could read her lists.

Caleb paced behind the sofa, looking over her shoulder as she wrote. She was glad she didn't have to look him in the eye and have this difficult conversation.

"I won't do it in a test tube. It's the natural way or no way."

Her pen froze. "I—" She'd expected artificial insemination. The thought of making love to Caleb again left her dizzy. "All right."

"How many attempts?"

She struggled to catch her breath at his businesslike approach to something so intimate. "It's unlikely I'll conceive the first time. Will you agree to keep trying for a year? That's the figure in our earlier contracts."

"Fine."

"When I give birth the land will be deeded over to you."

In her past relationships her partners had faulted her for scheduling their encounters. If it was so unromantic to plan ahead, then why did the prospect of penciling in a year's worth of sex with Caleb make her feel like she'd swallowed a hummingbird?

He stopped right behind her and braced his hands on the back of the couch. The hair on her nape stood up. "What if you don't get pregnant?"

She didn't even want to consider the possibility of failure. Of course, the longer it took, the more they'd have to try. Her pulse fluttered, and she cursed the rampant hormones making her body warm and damp. "Then one of us has a problem. I want children, Caleb. I guess I'd have to seek alternate means."

"With livestock we pay half up-front and half on live birth. If you don't conceive by the end of the year, I want to buy the land at a fair rate."

"And what do you do if the failure is the...stud's?"

He stopped pacing at the end of the couch and pinned her with his dark gaze. His face tightened. "All monies are returned and the contract is voided."

"I think that's appropriate in this case. If I don't conceive and the fault is mine, I'll sell you the land for the price I paid."

His chin thrust forward. "You paid too much."

She couldn't help smiling. "So Maria tells me, but my lawyer and my accountant don't agree."

"I want first right of refusal if you decide to sell the Double C between now and when you catch."

She wrote it down.

"How soon can we get it done?"

She flushed and tingled all over. Her nipples hardened beneath her silk gown and robe. She looked up from the list and her eyes met his. "I should ovulate next week. I keep track of my temperature to know the exact date."

His jaw clenched and unclenched. His gaze dropped to her breasts. He cleared his throat, shoved his hand through his hair and looked away. "The paperwork."

"Oh." Embarrassment warmed her face. "I could call my attorney and ask him to write up the agreement immediately."

"Do that. Get him to fax a draft so I can carry it to my own attorney."

She stood and offered her hand. It seemed peculiar to be shaking over such a personal promise. "We have a deal?"

"No matter what happens, I won't marry you."

She didn't want to marry him, either, so why did his rejection hurt? "I'm not expecting you to. Do we have a deal or not?"

"Yeah." He clasped her hand. Their gazes held and his heated. She thought he'd reach for her, but instead he released her hand quickly and let himself out the front door without another word.

Shaken by the unexpected encounter, Brooke collapsed on the sofa. He wanted her. As much as Caleb might deny it, his eyes didn't lie. None of the men from her past had ever looked at her with even a fraction of the passion in Caleb's dark gaze. Heaven help her, she wanted him more than she'd ever wanted any of her former lovers—even her fiancé—and that scared her.

Time for damage control. Beginning now, this was a business deal. She'd keep her emotions out of her relationship with Caleb. Otherwise, she could get used to having him by her side, and it didn't take a doctorate in psychology to know what would happen next. She'd learned the hard way too many times before.

Caleb was the last to enter the kitchen for the powwow Brooke had called. While the others were settling in their chairs he put his hands on her shoulders and bent to whisper, "You have that paperwork for me yet?"

She shifted away from his touch by scooting her chair forward. "Yes. Please sit down so we can get started."

He tried to ignore the way her scent had gone straight to his head…and other places. It was the first time she'd addressed the entire staff, and he attributed her starchy tone to nervousness for the meeting ahead. A pile of her books sat in the middle of the table and he knew what was coming—worse, he could guess the response she'd get. He sat down beside her and braced himself for the arguments.

She began with a smile, making eye contact with each person at the table except him. "I'd like for you all to become familiar with my self-actualization strategies and incorporate them into your jobs here at the Double C."

Openmouthed silence greeted her statement. Maria voiced the first protest. "You want us to read all these books?"

The others grumbled and shifted in their seats. Caleb

felt the need to speak up. "It's an awful lot to swallow in just a few days, Brooke."

"Then take a week, but by the time the second group of guests arrives I'd like for everyone to have completed the reading, including you, Mr. Lander."

*Mr. Lander?* Whoa. He'd be lying if he said his pride wasn't stung by her response. There was nothing wrong with acting professional, but just hours ago they'd agreed to make a baby—the most intimate thing a man and woman could do together. He didn't expect to be treated like a hired hand.

"I've already read 'em, sweetheart."

Brooke bristled over the endearment, but he'd be damned if he'd sneak around in the dark of night and hide their relationship. Eyebrows would rise when folks realized he and Brooke were going to have a baby out of wedlock. He'd hate to see what the locals would make of the true agreement. For his kid's sake he hoped word never got out.

Toby griped, "Caleb, it's three whole books."

He'd known Toby since elementary school, and he knew the reason Toby spun such great cowboy tales was that he wasn't much of a reader.

He turned toward Brooke, his thigh nudging hers inadvertently beneath the table. Again she shifted away. "Brooke, the back cover says your books are available on tape. Why don't you order some? Might be a good idea to have 'em on hand to sell to guests anyway."

"I'll do that. In the meantime, I'll be wandering around studying what each of you do to find the best way to incorporate my theories." She stood, bringing their meeting to a close. "I'll see you all in the morning."

Zero enthusiasm greeted her statement.

Caleb spoke up. "Look, folks, it's not like she's asking you to convert the guests to a new religion. She's just trying to get everybody to approach tasks with a positive slant."

The ranch hands filed out and Brooke stepped in his path. "May I have a moment?"

Maria gave Caleb a sympathetic look and closed the door behind them. Brooke drew herself up to her full height and frowned at him. "Please don't touch me or call me sweetheart in front of the other employees. It's inappropriate."

His mind was stuck on the *other* employee part. "Let me get this straight. You expect me to crawl into your bed at night, but during the day I'm just another employee?"

She pressed her fingers to her temple. "Caleb, we agreed that neither of us is looking for anything permanent."

His temperature shot up a few degrees. "We're going to be sharing a kid. That's pretty damned permanent."

"Yes, but—"

"I've got news for you, lady. I'm not a test tube you can keep on ice until you're ready to use me."

She shifted on her feet and her skin pinked. She kept her gaze focused on his chin rather than meet his eyes. "I can see how you might feel that way, but it's best if we remember that this is a business arrangement."

Every single one of his muscles knotted. "In other words, you're paying me for sex on demand, like a gigolo you'd pick up on a street corner."

She held up her hands and then carefully laced her fingers. "It's not like that at all. I just want to keep my life in order. Business and pleasure don't mix."

Was she for real? "And you think you can turn off the heat we generate just because you want to?"

"Of course." She looked so darned certain he just had to prove her wrong. No, he *would* prove her wrong.

He stepped closer, trapping her between the counter and the refrigerator. She folded her arms, but he could see by the flush on her cheeks and the rapid rise and fall of her breasts that he was getting to her. Moving very deliberately he braced his arms on either side of her and leaned closer.

Her breath caught. She worried her lower lip with her teeth. There was no way she could ignore the attraction between them fourteen hours a day.

"I have news for you, *sweetheart.* I'm the best you've ever had. Don't think for one minute that you can forget that."

God knows he couldn't forget how good they were together.

Brooke's knees nearly dissolved. She swallowed hard and forced herself to breathe through her nose rather than gasp for air. Caleb's scent immediately filled her senses.

She cleared her throat and straightened her shoulders, struggling to get back to business. Once she had a measure of control, she forced herself to look him in the eye. "My attorney faxed a draft of our agreement. Would you like to see it?"

Caleb mashed his lips together, obviously displeased that she hadn't swooned at his feet. It was a good thing he had no idea how close she'd come.

He pushed off the counter, giving her the necessary breathing room. "Let's see it."

She led the way to the office. If her steps were hasty it wasn't because she was running from the man or the feelings he evoked. She needed to get back to work on her book, but she couldn't do that until she got this cowboy out of her house and out of her head.

# Nine

"Caleb? Maria said you were looking for me?"

At the sound of Brooke's voice he turned away from the bullpen and nearly groaned aloud. When Maria said Brooke was out, he'd assumed she meant in the car, but Brooke must have been exercising somewhere outside. The sun had kissed her cheeks and nose and her hair was windblown, giving her a sexy just out of bed look. Snug black shorts displayed her curvy hips to perfection and her sports bra left her midriff bare. He wanted to peel the tight-fitting garments off.

His blood stirred, knowing in a few days he'd be tracing the winding path again with his hands and lips. Of course, the reason he'd be touching her knotted his muscles up all over again. Making a baby and being responsible for one scared the hell out of him.

Evidently he wasn't the only one having trouble staying away from Brooke. Rico stopped at her heels. Darned if he didn't look like he'd had a bath and a good brushing. "Hey, boy. Where've you been?"

"Jogging with me. Where did those ugly beasts come from?" She shrunk away from the two retired bucking bulls Brand had convinced Charlie to buy a few years back.

Obviously she still hadn't read the file on what she'd bought. "They're yours. We've been keeping 'em at Crooked Creek."

"And why would I want them?"

"Some of your vacation cowboys like to try their hands at bull riding."

"Bull riding is listed in the brochure, but since I hadn't noticed any bulls during my morning runs I thought it had been terminated. Is it really something we want to continue? The liability alone must be horrendous."

"It's popular, besides Toby is a trained paramedic, and these guys are so old, they aren't likely to hurt anybody." Outside of the chutes the old guys were pretty docile. As if to prove his point Shotgun meandered over to have his head scratched. Not one to be left out, Hammer followed.

Brooke stepped away from the fence. "Aren't they dangerous?"

"Used to be back when Brand was riding them. Hammer is the bull Brand rode to lock in his first National Finals Rodeo win. Shotgun was Brand's first bounty bull win."

"What is a bounty bull?"

"One that hasn't been ridden in a real long time. The owners or sponsors put money on him for each buck off. The more cowboys the bull unloads the more money in the bank for the cowboy who finally makes the count.

"See, a champion bull has his pride. He gets tired of losing, and he'll get to the point that he won't let anyone defeat him by riding him again—even if it means hurting a cowboy to prevent it."

Her eyes widened, but he didn't think she realized she

and the bulls had something in common. Brooke was just as determined to keep a man from getting too close. Her idiot exes had put her on the defensive.

"And we want them here?"

"Brooke, these guys are too old to rodeo, no longer fertile, not tender enough for steak. If you sell 'em they'll become dog food. Trust me, Shotgun and Hammer are the kind of slow motion critters our dudes can hang onto for a couple of seconds."

She chewed on her bottom lip the way he wanted to. He took a step forward, but she stiffened and stepped away. Rico growled.

Rejected by the woman and the dog. His pride took a hit. How could she so easily dismiss the chemistry between them? He sure as hell couldn't seem to get it out of his mind. He'd gotten so he needed a daily dose of her company.

He shook his head to clear it. "The bulls weren't what I needed to ask you about. Let's head for the barn."

He led the way and she came along with the dog at her side. He stepped into the dark barn. It took a couple of seconds for his eyes to adjust enough to notice none of the crew was inside.

"Over here." He tugged on the sheet draping a white sofa. "What do you want to do with all this?"

"It's the furniture from my apartment."

He'd figured as much. "I need the barn. We usually set up the trampoline and ping-pong tables in here. Rainy day activities for the little folks. Besides, your furniture will be rat bedding if you leave it here."

She scanned the floor looking like she might jump up on the sofa if she spotted a rodent. "We have rats?"

"You will have if you keep all this nice, soft nesting material around." If she couldn't handle rats, he didn't even want to mention the other things that might like to curl up in this stack. Rico knew. He took off to sniff around for critters.

"Where can I put my things? There isn't room in the house." She didn't quite meet his gaze.

"Yard sale."

Her eyes widened in horror. She stroked a hand over the back of a chair upholstered in flowery fabric. "I don't want to sell it."

"Planning on using it again?"

"I might."

Women grew attached to the damnedest things. None of the sheet-covered furniture looked like it could withstand the weight of a grown man. As far as he could tell it was all prissy, girly stuff, but her refusal to unload it was a reminder that she was likely to be a temporary fixture here. They'd make this baby and then God knows where he'd have to go to keep tabs on his child. On Brooke. "I'll see if I can find a place for it."

"Thank you. Caleb, I hate to ask a stupid question, but why are plastic cow heads hanging all over that wall?"

"Roping lessons." He pulled one down and shoved the shaft in a bale of straw. "Presto, it's a steer."

Her eyebrows rose. "Why would anyone want to rope a bale of hay?"

"Easier to learn on a target that's not moving."

"Oh, please. It would be as simple as horseshoes."

One thing he'd admired about Brooke was that she never backed down from a challenge. As the oldest of four kids, he excelled at issuing them. Sometimes it had been the only way to get chores done.

He nudged back his hat. "Bet you can't."

Sure enough she straightened up, narrowed her eyes and lifted her chin. Her gaze met his directly for the first time since she'd entered the barn. "Get me a rope."

Fighting a grin, he stepped into the tack room, found what he needed and offered it to her.

She studied the lariat, uncoiled it and then wound it back up. "How many chances do I get?"

He shrugged. The woman didn't understand the meaning of the word fail. He had to admire that. "As many as it takes."

Brooke whirled the rope around, but her technique was wrong. He could tell she wouldn't be roping anything anytime soon, but watching her swivel those hips was damned entertaining.

With her face contorted in concentration, she tried and missed five times, not even coming close. For some danged reason her fierce deliberation on twirling the rope reminded him how hard she tried at everything—even making love. Getting her to loosen up was half the battle. And once she did… He started to sweat, just thinking about how much Brooke could loosen up.

She sighed. "Okay, so it's not as easy as horseshoes."

"First lesson's free." His hands tingled with the anticipation of touching her, because he wasn't dumb enough to pass up this opportunity.

She held out the rope and he took it. Usually he just demonstrated, but he wanted to rattle her business-only attitude and get her to acknowledge that she was as aware of him as he was of her.

He stepped in close behind her, placed his left palm on her bare midriff, and aligned his hips with hers. Her skin was soft, her belly firm. He leaned closer, inhaling the scent of her shampoo, enjoying the warmth of her body against his. His throat—among other things—tightened up, and the urge to pull her close and just hold her nearly overwhelmed him.

He bent his head to speak softly into her ear. "It's all in the motion. You have to find your rhythm."

Her breath hitched and he knew he had her distracted. Good. He wasn't the only one.

Reaching around her with his right arm, he covered her hand with his and adjusted her grasp on the rope. He raised the loop over their heads and started the windup, but like when they danced, she tried to lead. "Ease up and do what I do. Draw circles. The loop will go wherever you tell it to. We're going to let go on three."

When her arm relaxed he counted and tossed. The rope settled over the plastic horns. She tipped her head to the side and stared at the bum steer like she was replaying the toss.

The curve of her neck tempted him. He bent his head and nipped the sensitive cord of her neck the way he knew she liked.

She shot out of his arms like a bullet from a gun. "What are you doing?"

"Teaching you to use that thing." He nodded toward the rope.

"No, you're not." Rico came to a sliding stop beside her. Brooke scratched the dog's ears without breaking eye contact.

Hooking his thumbs through his belt loops, he tried for a serious expression. "Then what am I doing?"

"You're anticipating our agreement."

She'd drawn a line he was determined to erase. "You're saying I can't touch you unless it's scheduled in that book of yours? 'Cause I have news for you, sweetheart. If I wanted to lay you on that prissy sofa of yours and *anticipate our agreement,* you wouldn't be complaining."

She blushed and bristled. "We have days before it's time."

He winked. "Maybe I need a little practice."

She snorted and rolled her eyes. "I don't think so."

He ought to be flattered. Instead he was just frustrated. Brooke wanted him and was determined to deny them both. And she'd turned the dog against him. "You need to loosen up that choke chain you're wearing around your neck before it strangles you."

"I beg your pardon?"

"What happened to the woman I had fun with in that hotel room and out on the range?"

She blanched. "I told you that wanton woman wasn't me. My life is complicated, Caleb. I'm juggling a writing career, a speaking career, now a dude ranch and soon, I hope, a family. I don't want to muddy the waters by mixing them."

"Life doesn't fit in neat little boxes, Brooke. You have to integrate it all or you'll end up dropping some of those balls you're juggling."

"And what would a rancher know about managing multiple careers?" The sarcasm in her voice stung.

She'd hit a nerve. He ground his teeth then forced himself to relax. "Ranching isn't rocket science, but it's pretty damned close. A rancher combines animal husbandry, land management, market shares and a whole cocktail of other ingredients to determine his bottom line."

"I'm sorry. I didn't realize ranching was so complicated."

"If you stick around long enough you'll figure it out. And what in the hell have you done to my dog?"

"According to the auction list, he's my dog. Aren't you, boy?" She knelt down to pet the mutt. Rico rolled onto his back and whimpered in ecstasy when she scratched his belly.

In a couple more days, he'd be the one flat on his back writhing in ecstasy, but for now, he was jealous of a damned mutt.

Caleb surveyed their first group of guests and knew there'd be trouble.

The problem wouldn't come from the three families or the two couples. While the college girls would be a distraction for some of the younger male staff members, the group of four thirty-something bankers from Toledo would be his biggest headache. They'd zeroed in on Brooke the minute she'd stepped onto the porch, eyeing her like a wolf eyes a spring calf.

The bankers were more her type than he was, and they seemed more interested in Brooke's motivational mumbo jumbo than the dude ranch experience they'd paid for. If that weren't enough aggravation they'd reserved rooms in the main house rather than a cabin.

His territorial hackles rose. He and Brooke had signed the paperwork closing their deal this morning. Brooke was his, at least until the job was done, and he wouldn't share.

The minute those city yahoos had started eyeing her he'd decided he couldn't leave her alone in the wolf's den. For better or worse, he'd move into the main house for the remainder of the week.

His blood ran hot with anticipation of making love to Brooke again and cold with fear of the deal blowing up in his face. He liked Brooke. Too much sometimes.

The guests gathered round. Caleb gave the welcome spiel he usually gave Charlie's guests. He was distracted by Brooke wearing a short, flirty purple skirt and by the bankers with their howl-at-the-moon mind-set. He must have managed to get through the welcome coherently because folks laughed at the right spots.

He introduced Brooke and the crew and sent the guests off to their cabins to settle in. They'd meet again in an hour for the opening day poolside barbecue.

He planned to stick to Brooke like a cocklebur. Tomorrow he was supposed to take a group out riding, but he sure as hell wasn't going to leave her here with the bankers—even if it meant he had to sit in on her motivational pep talk.

He'd rather eat worms.

He flagged Brooke down on the back porch. "I gotta run home for a minute. I'll be back before the barbecue."

"Is something wrong?"

"Nope. Just need to pack a few things. I've decided to stay here the first few nights in case there are problems." The only problems he anticipated were related to the bankers sniffing around Brooke.

"Where will you stay? The cabins and the upstairs rooms are full."

"Charlie has a guest room in the private quarters. I've stayed there before."

Brooke put a hand to her throat. "I'm staying in the guest room."

Oh hell. "Why aren't you in the master bedroom?"

"I was, but Rico kept circling the bed and whining. So we moved into the guest room."

He could kiss sleep goodbye now that he knew Brooke had been in that bed.

"You changed rooms because Rico missed Charlie?" It wasn't love squeezing his heart. He didn't know *what* it was, but it sure as hell wasn't that.

"Well, yes, and because the bed is—" A flush climbed her cheeks. She looked away. "—too big."

It wasn't too big for two. He lov—*liked* the way she blushed and had to stuff his hand in his pocket to keep from stroking her hot cheek. "Mind if I use it then?"

"I…no. We'll have to share when it's time to…"

Thoughts of tangling the sheets with Brooke sent desire swirling through his blood like a dust devil. He'd get that playful side of her to come back or die trying. "Right."

From the back porch Brooke looked over the gathering on the patio. Caleb and the crew had done this countless times before and it showed. She was the only one who didn't know her role.

Country music filled the air. A few guests swam. Others played volleyball in the sandpit beside the pool area. In another corner of the yard guests and staff whirled around on a wooden deck.

Caleb danced with one of their guests, a college girl who'd obviously already fallen for his cowboy charm if the dimples and fluttering eyelashes were anything to go by.

Never one to delude herself, Brooke identified the emotion mingling with her usual pre-event butterflies as jealousy. Caleb's job as manager and host demanded that he do his part to teach guests to two-step or line dance, but this morning he'd signed an agreement to father her child and, frankly, it bothered her to see another woman in his arms.

So she tortured herself by watching, but Caleb kept plenty of space between his body and the nubile young woman's. Additionally his gaze kept straying to the other guests, as if he were more concerned with keeping tabs on the evening's progress than on making time with another woman. Not once did he look deep into the girl's eyes and give her that knee-weakening sideways grin.

Gathering her courage, Brooke plastered a smile on her face and waded into the crowd hoping to find people interested in finding the winners within themselves. It took her only minutes to discover the majority of these people didn't want to talk about goals. They were more interested in trail rides and cowboy rituals—both of which she knew next to nothing about. Only the men from Ohio promised to attend her workshop tomorrow morning.

A warm hand descended on her shoulder. She didn't have to see Caleb to identify him. Her body remembered his touch and his scent. Besides, who else invaded her space with such regularity?

"You okay?" His breath stirred her hair.

"Mmm. The uniforms are a surprise." She answered without looking at him. Thoughts of the nights to come had her jittery enough. Her body grew damp whenever she allowed herself to count the hours until their next intimate encounter.

"Charlie always had the staff wear matching shirts on opening day. Makes us easy to find. I decided to stick with it. It's gimmicky, but…" His chest brushed her back as he shrugged.

He was close, so close she had to fight the urge to lean into him and draw from his strength while she battled nervousness over this evening and the week to come. She'd never had anyone to lean on before, but she was beginning to suspect that Caleb would be a strong and willing shoulder should she ever allow herself the weakness of depending on others.

She made the mistake of looking at him. He'd dressed the same as the staff in blue jeans and red checked shirt. He'd even tied a red bandanna around his throat, but he didn't look at all gimmicky. When she'd spotted him earlier her first thought had been that he looked roguish and sexy, like a hero from an old Western movie, the kind who always got the girl.

And in the nights to come she'd be that girl. The prospect left her breathless.

Gathering her composure, she said, "This isn't the first time you've welcomed the Double C's guests."

He dropped his hand from her shoulder and flexed his jaw. "Charlie needed help. I needed the money."

"You kept his books, dealt with his crew and managed his horses. How long had you been helping Charlie?"

His reluctance to elaborate was obvious. He folded his arms and rocked back on his heels. "A couple of years."

"So you know more about the dude ranch operation than you led me to believe."

"I never told you what I know."

His knowledge of the business hadn't been the biggest surprise of the evening. "You're a gifted speaker."

He turned his attention to the crowd, but she didn't miss the flush creeping up his neck. "I wouldn't say that."

"Your safety rules came across loud and clear and you made them laugh. Trust me, they'll remember your words." It had taken her years to master the confidence he'd displayed.

He shrugged off her praise.

"You should develop your talent, Caleb."

"Right. I'll practice on the cattle."

"Good communicative skills can carry you places."

"There's no place else I want to be. My friends and family are here."

The man was in a rut and didn't even know it. If anyone needed to attend her workshop, it was Caleb. "Complacency never yields success."

"Success by whose standards?"

She sighed. Arguing with him wasn't how she wanted to spend her first day in her new business, but it frustrated her that he didn't want to utilize his talent. "You're good, Caleb. I could help you take your oratorical skills to the next level."

"That's what my ex said—only in smaller words—right before she asked me to choose between her and Crooked Creek."

And he'd chosen the ranch. Another thought occurred to her. She pursed her lips and tilted her head. "Are you afraid of success?"

"What?" He stared at her as if she'd spouted nonsense.

"Some people sabotage their futures because they fear the expectations and resultant pressures success levies on them."

He muttered a few words under his breath. She thought he might be swearing. "Don't psychoanalyze me, Doc. You're the one reevaluating your life, not me."

"Perhaps you should."

He practically bristled with anger. "I agreed to get you pregnant. I didn't marry you. So quit trying to change me."

"Is that what your ex-wife did? Try to change you?"

"Brooke, don't go there." The timbre of his voice deepened to a warning growl.

What had the woman done to make him so defensive?

One of the Ohio men broke away from the crowd and crossed the patio, stopping in front of her.

"Teach me to two-step, Brooke?"

Caleb's arm clamped around her waist. Her breath

caught and her pulse fluttered at the unexpected and possessive gesture.

"Sorry, buddy. Brooke's promised this one to me." Caleb signaled to one of the women who helped Maria around the house and she headed their way. "Jan will teach you."

Caleb threaded his fingers through Brooke's and pulled her onto the wooden deck. She didn't protest since she had more to say on his lack of ambition, but then he pulled her close—closer than he had that night at the restaurant and her questions vanished. His hand definitely hadn't rested so low on her hip. The warmth permeating the fabric of her skirt wreaked havoc on her ability to think rationally or concentrate on the steps.

They'd made a couple of awkward passes around the deck before he spoke. "Brooke, look at me and relax."

She jerked her head up and clipped his chin. "Sorry."

They completed another circle around the floor. "You have the basic steps down. Get ready because I'm going to lift my arm and you're going to turn under it. Ready. Go."

She tried, lost count of her steps and ended up stumbling against him.

"We're not doing that again," he said in a tight voice against her temple.

She wrinkled her nose, determined not to let one failure stop her. "Give me another chance. I messed up."

"No, sweetheart, you didn't, but when you twirled your skirt spun out and I could almost see your panties. My sap's running high already just knowing we're going to be making love in four days."

Her muscles locked and her feet refused to move. She became aware of others' questioning expressions and led Caleb off the dance floor into an unoccupied corner of the backyard.

"Caleb, I thought you understood how the fertility cycle works. I ovulate in four days. For optimum odds of conception we should make love before then. Preferably more than once.''

Desire flashed in Caleb's eyes and then his jaw tensed. ''So why've you been pulling away each time I touch you?''

''Because I won't be fertile for another forty-eight hours.''

He nudged back his hat and parked his hands on his hips. ''We're arguing over *hours?*''

''We're not arguing. I am simply stating that we need to make love twelve and twenty-four hours before ovulation. Any other time would be a wasted effort.''

The pleat between his brows told her she'd angered him. Perhaps *wasted* effort wasn't the best choice of words.

''Tell you what, boss, you send me a memo stating the time and the place and I'll see if I can work it into my schedule.'' Caleb turned on his heel and stalked off.

Cold showers weren't his thing, but right after the guests had returned to their cabins Caleb had dived into one.

He stared at the business card he'd tossed on the bathroom counter. Brooke had written two dates and times on the back of one of her cards and slipped it to him at dinner. Being penciled in like some damned doctor's appointment shouldn't turn him on, but it did.

If it had the same effect on Brooke she hadn't shown it during the after dinner cowboy tales. But it would. He'd make sure of it.

He finished drying his face and wrapped a towel around his hips. Anticipation of driving her slam out of her mind flowed through his bloodstream like a straight shot of tequila on an empty stomach.

He'd get her so hot and bothered she couldn't wait until her scheduled time.

''Wasted effort my a—''

A noise in the hall drew his attention. He opened the door expecting to find Brooke. Instead he found one of the bankers. Even though it wasn't an emotion he'd dealt with before, it didn't take Caleb long to identify the unfamiliar burn in his gut as jealousy. "You lost, Ron?"

"Oh, ah, hey, Caleb. I'm looking for Brooke. I ah…wanted her to clarify something about tomorrow's workshop."

The guy was lying through his perfectly capped teeth. Caleb fought the urge to loosen some of those caps with his fists. The man was a guest. One thing Charlie had instilled in him was to treat all guests—even the ones determined to cheat on their wives—with respect.

"These are *our* private quarters. You must've missed the sign on the door. I'll tell Brooke to make time for your questions tomorrow."

The guy went bug-eyed. "*You* and *Brooke?*"

"Yep." Was it so hard to believe?

"You're not the type I'd expect a successful woman like Brooke to hook up with."

Caleb said nothing. He knew Ron was right.

"I guess I'll see you in the morning then."

Caleb followed him to the door and locked it after him.

"I thought you said we didn't need to lock our doors," Brooke said from behind him.

He turned and spotted her in the open doorway to her bedroom. Any calming effect his cold shower might have provided evaporated. She wore the same silky robe she'd worn in the hotel. Her long legs were bare, and God help him, he didn't think she had a stitch on beneath the thin fabric.

His body responded predictably. He cleared his throat and tried to remember what they were talking about. "That's with locals. Outsiders, especially the cheating-on-the-wife-kind, are a different story. When there are guests in the house keep the door to your private quarters locked. Day and night."

Her gazed drifted over him, lingering on his pectorals before traveling down his legs and back up to his face. She might as well have been stroking him with her hands given the way his body responded. It was only a matter of time before she realized how the hunger in her eyes aroused him. It wasn't like the towel would conceal the result of his detoured blood flow.

She wet her lips, exhaled slowly and jerked her gaze to the leather organizer she held in her hands. He liked knowing she wasn't as unaffected as she wanted to be. "We have a big day planned for tomorrow. We should turn in."

"Do you write everything in that notebook?"

"Just about. It helps me clarify my thoughts and focus on the desired outcomes. I never leave home without it."

"Like a security blanket."

She frowned. "It's a tool, not a crutch."

"Sweetheart, if you can't get through a day without it then it's no different than an addiction." He moved closer and leaned his arm against the doorjamb beside her head. "Did you write down what we'd be doing in a couple of nights?"

She stiffened up. "I have our time blocked off."

"Did you write that I'm going to start with tasting your little toe and work my way slowly up to your mouth?"

Her breath hitched. "I don't think that's necessary."

"The next morning I'm going to join you in the shower. After I work up a good lather I'll spread it over your body. Then I'm gonna press you up against the wall and slide so deep inside you that you'll make that sexy little noise I like so much."

Her breathing quickened. She swallowed. "Yes, well—"

"Do you know what I'm going to do tonight? I'm gonna lay in that big bed and dream about you and me doing the things we did in the hotel."

She squeezed her eyes shut and he grinned.

"I'm gonna think about the two of us skinny-dipping in the pool and making out on the steps in the shallow end."

A sound erupted from her throat. She tried to cover it by coughing.

"I'm gonna think about spreading you over Charlie's desk..."

She looked like she might hyperventilate.

"...and the kitchen table."

Every muscle in her body tensed up and the pulse at the base of her throat fluttered faster.

"I might even think about us on the porch swing on the patio outside my room.

"I know I'll be thinking about us in that deep whirlpool bath. Do you know the jets are placed exactly right for—"

"Good night," she squeaked, and then she slammed her bedroom door in his face.

It was a good thing she did because his blood pressure couldn't take any more erotic talk. His little exercise in heating her up had nearly caused him to have a meltdown. Turning on his heel, he headed for his second cold shower of the night. But he was grinning every step of the way.

# Ten

The next morning Caleb settled back in the club chair, eager to see Brooke in action during her first motivational workshop.

He knew she'd probably be disappointed by the low turnout. The only attendees besides himself were the bankers from Toledo and a retiree from Tennessee.

He'd read her books, but it all seemed like common sense to him. Make a plan. Go for it. Work hard and you'll get there eventually. He'd learned it at his daddy's knee.

Brooke came in and he wanted to pop the bankers upside their heads when they returned her smile with sappy ones of their own. When her gaze skated past his her smile faltered.

"I hope you all had a relaxing ride this morning, because for the next hour we're going to take a crash course on how to tap the winner within us all. I warn you that this is just an introductory workshop. You'll have opportunities throughout the week to study more in-depth methods of goal actualization.

"Now, before you can win you have to know what you want. On the pad in front of you write down the one thing you want most."

Caleb picked up his pad and wrote *You.*

Brooke paced around the room, reading over everyone's shoulder as she talked about goals and narrowing down your focus. "Next you need to set a time frame. When do you think you can realistically get what you—" she'd stopped behind him "—want."

He wrote *Tonight.*

Brooke cleared her throat and moved on. Caleb fought a grin.

"It's all right if you're looking five or ten years down the road, or even as far as retirement. Now, break down your goal into smaller components and estimate the time you need to achieve each step."

He jotted down pieces of her clothing in the order he'd like to remove them and approximately how many seconds each would take.

"Now write down what's stopping you from reaching that goal."

She paused behind him again and he thought he heard her wheeze.

He wrote *cooperation.*

"Your goal should never depend on someone else. It should be something you alone can accomplish." Her voice was a little breathless.

"In other words, choosing to sell the next great American novel is out of your control because you can't control the publishing industry, but you can choose to *write* the next great novel."

Caleb sat up straighter. "So you're saying that if my goal is to have a kid before I'm forty, I need to change it because it depends on others."

He could see his question hit the target by the way she

blanched. ''Not necessarily. You can become a parent by other means. Sometimes you need to think outside the box and approach from a different perspective. When a door refuses to open look around for another door or perhaps a window of opportunity.

''Failure is okay. As a matter of fact, Henry Ford considered failure an opportunity to start over with more information. Find out why you failed, correct it and try again. The one thing successful people have in common is that they don't quit.''

One of the bankers said, ''Those who try the most can expect to fail the most.''

Brooke gave a sympathetic shrug. ''That's the way it usually works out, I'm afraid. Greatness is never achieved without great effort. Mistakes happen. Success is more than a destination. It's the journey. It's what you learn along the way. The only way you truly fail is if you learn nothing at all and keep making the same mistakes over and over.''

He'd made the mistake of caring about a woman before. Was he repeating his failures? Brooke was certainly growing on him. Was a relationship with her destined to fail the way his with Amanda had, or had he learned a few new tricks over the years?

''Now, look at what you've written. Revise, if necessary. Decide what you're willing to give up in order to realize your goal.''

Caleb's pencil remained still. What was he willing to give up for Brooke? Was he willing to forfeit anything to get her back in his bed?

Was his bed the only place he wanted her? No.

He liked her grit and the way she tackled a challenge head-on. But he wanted the woman who hadn't been afraid of letting go. Regardless of what she'd said about not fearing failure, Brooke held back more than anybody he knew.

What would it take to set her free? Caleb interrupted

again. "Your book said success is something you feel inside. No one else can give it to you. So if you're happy doing what you're doing, you're successful—even if others don't think so."

She bit her lip. "I believe you could argue that point. Success should be internal. If your goal is something external, then you'd need to look deeper to discover what it represents to you internally. For example, if you want to be a millionaire, it's probably because you believe the money will bring you security. If you want to buy land, you have to discover what the land really means to you."

He took her comment personally. It was hard not to when she was looking him in the eye. What did buying back the Double C mean to him? It wasn't like Crooked Creek would fold without it. He had the money he'd saved to buy Double C invested. It could carry them through plenty of lean years.

It was the guilt. One night he'd screwed up, had too much to drink and allowed himself to become trapped in a bad situation. His family had paid the price for his stupidity and they'd never laid one word of blame at his door. His mistake had cost Brand his college fund and forced his little brother into a rodeo career he hadn't wanted. They'd lost half their homestead because he hadn't been man enough to stop Amanda from blowing every dime they had.

Hell, he hadn't even made her prove her pregnancy before putting the ring on her finger and the noose around his neck.

His throat was tight. "What if you've made mistakes and others had to pay the price?"

She rested a soothing hand on his shoulder and gave his tight muscles a squeeze. "We all make bad choices and you have to forgive yourself for those and move on. Sometimes damage control is appropriate, but sometimes you just have to walk away."

The expression in her eyes said she understood and she

didn't blame him. His chest tightened and his throat and eyes burned.

Brooke continued around the room. "You have the basic strategy. I'll be happy to answer any questions you might have."

Caleb bolted. He needed time to digest what he'd discovered. All these years he'd blamed Amanda for his troubles when the blame rested squarely on his own shoulders.

Brooke stared out the bathroom window at the moonlit sky. It was the first moment of solitude she'd had since this morning when Caleb, a nonbeliever in her theories, had made her doubt everything she'd ever written, everything she'd ever taught with a few probing questions. How she'd managed to get through the remainder of the workshop she'd never know.

She wanted her mother's approval. She wanted public credibility. She wanted a baby. Her goals were both external and dependent on others. She—who'd known what she wanted and how she was going to get it since the age of thirteen—needed a serious reevaluation.

She was debating her problem when she heard a knock on the door. It had to be Caleb because she'd locked the door to the private quarters when she'd returned after dinner. Only she, Caleb and Maria had keys and Maria had gone home.

She left the water running in the bathtub and slipped on her robe. As expected, Caleb stood on the other side when she opened the door. The sight of him made her breath catch. The knowledge that tomorrow night they'd make love—unless she changed her mind—made her ache.

A frown of concern puckered his forehead. "Are you all right? You were pretty quiet at dinner."

How could she admit that the very theories she'd based her career on were in doubt? "I'm fine."

"Do I hear water running?"

"I'm getting ready to take my bath."

A smile lifted the corner of his mouth. "Need some help?"

Heat raced through her. "No, thanks. I—I'm not ready for company."

His hot gaze slid over her slowly, thoroughly. "You look ready to me."

"I have to shave my legs and get ready for tomorrow night." There, that ought to run him off.

"I shave every day. I'm experienced. Let me help."

Dear heavens. "I might not be fertile now."

"So?"

There was no doubt that she wanted him. This morning his goal chart had rattled her so badly it was a miracle she'd been able to remember what she was supposed to say next.

She had no idea what to say now. She wanted to keep business and pleasure separate, but he seemed determined to stop her.

He stepped forward. She stepped back. The next thing she knew they were standing in the bathroom and she had no recollection of making the decision to let him join her. Flustered, she turned off the tap.

He stroked a hand over his evening beard. "You have a spare razor? I'd hate to give you razor burn."

A flock of hummingbirds took flight in her stomach. "Yes."

When she faced Caleb again with the disposable razor in her hand he was sitting on the closed toilet removing his boots and socks. He stood and reached for his belt buckle.

She froze. "Why are you undressing?"

"My clothes are too dirty to wash 'em in the same water we're going to wash you."

She'd expected they'd make love after her bath. It looked like he planned to do so during. The man never ceased to make her step out of her comfort zone. She chewed her lip. Was that necessarily a bad thing?

He undressed and stepped into the oversize tub like he'd done this a dozen times before.

Jealousy wasn't a feeling she enjoyed. "Have you ever shaved a woman's legs?"

"Nope, but I'm a fast learner." He offered her a hand.

She had to be out of her mind. Brooke took a deep breath, untied her robe and let it drop to the floor. She heard Caleb's sharply indrawn breath and put her hand in his.

"Sit there and lean back." He sat down facing her with the spigot at his back, bent his long legs and spread his knees. The water wasn't deep enough to hide his arousal. Her skin turned hot and flushed all over and it had nothing to do with the temperature of the water.

"Can you hold this?" He offered her the hand mirror she kept on the vanity.

He had her so frazzled she hadn't even noticed him picking it up. With trembling hands she held the mirror. He reached for the bar of soap and created a froth in his big hands.

She recalled the words he'd used to torment her last night. He'd said he'd spread lather all over her and then he'd slide deep inside her. Right now, her insides were one tight achy knot of anticipation.

He soaped his face and shaved in short, swift strokes. She'd watched men shave before, but it had never been the erotic experience it was now. Of course, they hadn't been naked and sharing her tub. Nor had they been shaving off the stubble to protect her sensitive skin.

He took the mirror from her and laid it on the bathroom floor. After rinsing his face he reached for the soap again. A shiver of expectancy shimmied over her as the bubbles formed in his hands and the heat built in his eyes.

He soaped and massaged the bottom of her right foot, working his way past her ankle to her calf and past her knee. He didn't stop until he reached the waterline. Resting her foot on his shoulder, he reached for the razor and slid it slowly up her leg. Her nerve endings crackled in his wake.

In this open and exposed posture she should have been uncomfortable. Instead, the hot promise in his eyes made her feel like the sexiest woman on the planet which she definitely was not.

With stroke after deliberate stroke he removed the foam to midthigh. The torture started anew when he started over on her left leg. Somehow she managed to endure the experience without moaning aloud by closing her eyes and concentrating very hard. It wasn't easy. Pleasure mounted until her blood seemed effervescent.

"Sit on the side."

Her eyes flew open. "Excuse me?"

"Bikini line. Sit on the side. I'll finish up." The tense expression on his face belied his casual tone of voice.

Dear heavens. Her muscles trembled as she lifted herself to the edge of the tub.

Caleb reached for the bar of soap and worked up a lather. She'd swear he procrastinated just to torment her. Finally he spread the bubbles over the tops and backs of her legs with long, slick swipes.

He shaved the outside of her legs before parting her thighs and soaping her right up to her panty line. He lingered, teased, and titillated, but avoided the part of her screaming for his touch.

She'd never been so turned on in her entire life, and she couldn't wait to see what he'd do next. And then it hit her. Caleb had her anticipating stepping out of her comfort zone rather than fearing the consequences. He'd changed her.

He slid the razor closer and closer to the needy part of her. For one teensy moment she recalled a fantasy she'd once read about and wondered if Caleb would stop at her panty line. She had her answer when he laid down the razor and unplugged the drain. She nearly slid back into the water.

"What are you doing?" she asked, even though it was obvious the most erotic experience of her life was over. His thick erection told her they'd still make love, but it would be in the bed. Disappointment washed over her. *She,* who didn't have a spontaneous bone in her body, wanted to leap into the unknown. But only with Caleb. He was her life raft. With him she could swim in uncharted waters without fear of drowning.

He pulled her to her feet, reached for the handheld shower nozzle and turned it on. After adjusting the temperature and flow he aimed the nozzle at her. "Rinsing us off."

The water pulsed over her. He worked his way from her shoulders down her legs. Her already oversensitized skin ignited and she thought she'd spontaneously combust. Before she could gather the nerve to ask him to put her out of her misery, he'd shut off the shower and replugged the drain.

The tub began to fill. Her heart skipped a beat. "Now what are you doing?"

His gaze rasped over her, down to her toes and back up to her face. The blaze in his dark eyes sent her temperature soaring. "I'm going to lather you up and slide so deep inside you that you make that sexy noise that drives me wild."

Her knees almost buckled at his low, growling voice. She couldn't catch her breath.

He switched places with her, sat down and beckoned. "Straddle my legs. Sit on my…" He paused and winked.

She nearly swallowed her tongue.

"…knees."

She was out of control. She wanted to grab him and… She settled for grabbing the bar of soap before he could reach it and kneeling over him. She worked up a froth and then spread it over his chest, taking time to outline his erogenous zones in excruciating detail. It was only fair that she torment him the way he'd done her. All the while the visible proof of his arousal stood between them.

Caleb's nipples tightened beneath her fingertips and his stomach contracted. His thick shaft jerked when she lathered the dense hair surrounding it but stopped just short of wrapping her fingers around him. She peeked at him from beneath her lashes, noting the flush of arousal staining his cheekbones.

"You tease." The corner of his mouth turned up in a slow, sexy grin. He kicked the spigot, turning off the water even though it barely reached the tops of his thighs. The move pitched her forward and enabled him to snatch the soap out of her hands. He grinned wickedly. The glint in his eyes warned her that he was ready to wreak his own revenge for her teasing. He slowly, deliberately lathered his hands. She wet her lips. Anticipation quivered through her.

He cupped her shoulders and pulled her forward to capture her mouth in a kiss so ravenous she couldn't breathe, couldn't think, couldn't move. As a woman who aggressively molded her own future, it amazed her that she'd become putty in Caleb's hands and she liked it. He skated slippery palms over her back and down to her bottom, washing her thoroughly, intimately.

She nearly bit his tongue. She broke the kiss to inhale and stared at him in surprise. Each time she thought she'd learned everything Caleb had to teach her about her own body he carried her to a higher plateau. He glided his soapy hands over her breasts to thumb and roll her nipples. She couldn't remain silent any longer.

"That's it," he encouraged her. "Tell me how good my hands feel on you. Tell me where you want me to touch you next."

And she did. Words were her vocation and she used them shamelessly. He complied, stroking her until pleasure so intense she thought she'd faint rocketed through her.

Caleb pulled her forward to capture her cries and devour her mouth. He drew back a fraction, his nose touching hers, his gaze holding hers. "Ride me, Brooke."

Eagerly she moved over him, took him in her hand and slowly descended until he filled her completely. Caleb bucked beneath her, driving so deep she made the sound he'd promised she would, and she continued to make it over and over again with each thrust.

She rode him until her thighs burned from exertion, but need urged her on. He brushed the heart of her with one hand and cupped and caressed her breasts with the other. The ache inside her built to an unbearable point and then she tumbled into rapture so exquisite even her toes tingled.

Caleb's voice joined hers as he pulsed deep inside her.

And then all was silent except for sloshing water and gasping breaths. Spent and exhausted, she collapsed against his chest.

Caleb scooped warm water over her back. He nuzzled her hair and kissed her temple. His chest heaved beneath her.

And then it hit her. They'd made love without protection. For better or worse, the seed of their baby could have already been planted. Since this morning, when he'd cast doubt on her plans, she didn't know if that was a good thing or not.

They'd done it. Caleb's heart pounded harder instead of slowing. He could have given Brooke his baby.

So why did that zing in his blood feel more like anticipation than fear? After Amanda he'd sworn he'd never father a child. Hell, at one point he'd had an appointment to get a vasectomy, but he'd fallen off his danged horse the day before the planned procedure and broken his leg.

He'd had to cancel. He hadn't rescheduled. And now he was glad.

Goose bumps sprang up on Brooke's back beneath his water-wrinkled fingers. He nudged on the hot water with his toe and scooped water over her back. As cold as she must be Brooke dozed on his chest. He hated to wake her. She was so darned intense about everything, it wasn't often she let her guard down. He savored holding her, knowing that once the sensual haze cleared she'd put the barricades back up.

She was vulnerable although she'd never admit it. Tonight he'd caught her at a weak moment. He'd known all through dinner that something was bothering her and wondered if she realized that she didn't take her own advice. If anybody feared failing, it was Brooke. His protective instincts came out in full force when she tried to tough out a difficult situation.

He didn't need a college degree to know that her ex-lovers had hurt her and that she was scared to risk another relationship. Why else would she be trying to have a baby on her own? Why else would she push him away every time he got too close?

What he'd begun as a game to make her admit she couldn't wait until their scheduled encounter tomorrow night had blown up in his face. Sure, he could make her desire him, but when the haze of passion faded all she really wanted from him was his sperm—something she could easily get elsewhere.

And he was left wanting Brooke: her ditties, her determination and that spark in her eyes when she was ready to accept a challenge or get a little wild.

Today she'd handed him a key to the emotions that had driven him to work seventy hours a week for the past decade. He'd been beating himself up and he had to stop. He couldn't change his past, but he could look toward his future.

Would that future include Brooke and their child?

# Eleven

The phone jolted Brooke from a sound sleep. Caleb's arm pinned her to the mattress but she could move enough to reach the receiver. ''Double C.''

''Brooke, I have a job for you.'' Her agent's voice cleared the sleepy fog from her brain. ''Can you make an eleven o'clock flight to Miami?''

Shoving the hair out of her eyes, she sat up and glanced at the clock. It was *very* early considering how little sleep Caleb had allowed her last night. A smile tugged her lips. ''What's going on?''

Caleb stirred beside her. It didn't take a genius to translate the fire kindling in his eyes or the sexy grin. Her skin tingled in response. The man had kept her so busy in bed and out during the last three days she hadn't had time to deal with the cracks in her belief system. She captured his hand before it could travel any farther up her thigh.

''There's been a last-minute cancellation at the SuperMart convention. If you can make it, it's yours.''

She had time if she rushed, but could Caleb handle the dude ranch without her? ''Hold on, Kelly.''

She covered the mouthpiece. ''I'm needed in Miami for a couple of days, can you spare me here? It's an eleven o'clock flight.''

He looked disappointed and she waited for him to either beg her to stay or to take him along as her lovers had done. One had wanted to share her limelight. The other had resented her career.

''Do what you've got to do. I'll get somebody to cover for me so I can drive you to the airport and pick you up when you return.''

She blinked at him in surprise. Would the man ever do what she expected? ''I'll be there, Kelly. Can you make the arrangements for me?''

Brooke tried to concentrate while Kelly provided the hotel and flight information, but Caleb crawled from the bed naked and headed to the bathroom. She had to ask Kelly to repeat the information. She heard the tub filling.

Caleb came back into the room as she was hanging up. He reached for last night's jeans and pulled them on. ''I'll rustle up some breakfast while you take your bath.''

Brooke stared after him and then threw back the covers and hustled through her morning routine. She kept expecting Caleb to crawl into the tub with her or do something else to make her late. Instead she found him in the bedroom with her empty suitcase open on the bed.

''If you tell me what to pack I'll do it while you eat.''

She didn't know what to make of the offer. Contrarily she was almost disappointed that he didn't try to detain her, because she didn't want to leave. That frightened her. Her career had always come first before. ''Thank you, but I can handle it.''

He shrugged and sat down on the edge of the bed to watch her eat. ''Do you get last-minute calls often?''

''Not often. Usually engagements are planned months

in advance. Are you sure you don't have a problem with me going?"

"Nah, bed'll be lonely, but I can wait till you get back. It'll be one hell of a reunion." He grinned and winked.

Brooke nearly choked on her muffin. She wanted to hurry up and leave so that she could hurry up and return which was totally inappropriate. She wouldn't be fertile three days from now and there wouldn't be any reason for them to sleep together. She ignored the twinge of disappointment and sipped her juice.

Caleb had her so rattled she was having trouble remembering this was a business relationship. She wasn't getting attached to this brown-eyed, slow-talking cowboy. It's just that the relationship would end eventually and she wasn't very good at endings.

"You don't have to drive me, Caleb. I'll need the commute to get my thoughts and my speech together."

She needed to get back on track. With a few well-placed questions during her workshop he'd caused her to have serious doubts about her goal plan. She needed to figure out where she'd gone wrong and make another plan—a plan that didn't include a Texan by her side. And she needed to discover why the thought of a future without Caleb made her want an antacid.

Caleb couldn't keep the grin off his face as he reentered the room after seeing Brooke off. He surveyed the wreck they'd made of the bed last night and every night since their shared bath. Pillows and covers were scattered all over the place.

If Brooke wasn't pregnant, it wasn't for lack of trying. And he didn't think it was bragging to say she seemed eager to get back home. When she did return they needed to figure out where this relationship was headed. Somewhere along the way they'd taken a detour from their original plan.

He gathered the strewn clothes. They'd been careful

about their sleeping arrangements. Some things a man and woman wanted to keep private—especially when the deal was as convoluted as this one.

He hoped to change that soon enough. He'd decided he couldn't let Brooke go anytime soon. He'd happily stay on as dude ranch manager if she'd supply him with a lifetime supply of her little ditties and unrelenting optimism. He especially liked being the only one who knew how to make her cast off her inhibitions in bed.

He yanked the comforter up from where they'd kicked it off the end of the bed. Something hit the floor. He bent to investigate and found a leather-bound book lying open beside the bench at the foot of the bed.

Brooke's journal. She never left home without it.

He reached down to pick it up and his own name jumped off the page. Below his name were two columns: one titled *Assets* and the other *Liabilities*.

Normally he would respect someone's privacy, but seeing his faults laid out on paper beside the anonymous donor's assets kept him from closing the book. His muscles tensed and his stomach sank as he read the remarks beneath his name.

*Lacks ambition. Undereducated. Not well traveled. Rough around the edges. My parents wouldn't approve of him. Becoming involved with Caleb would be career suicide. My rival would have a field day if I ended up with an uneducated cowboy.*

*Caleb makes me lose control.*

His gut burned. His chest hurt. He hadn't measured up for the first two women in his life: his mother and his wife. Both had dumped him. Now Brooke found him lacking. As a man. As the father of her child.

It was obvious she believed the sperm donor a better candidate to father her child, so why had she chosen him? The need for answers drove him to turn the page. He found what he was looking for in her notes about a rival's comments on a radio talk show.

*Only achieving my goal of home and family will stop the vicious attacks,* she'd written.

*Problem: Dude ranch guests arriving. Must postpone insemination another month. Delay opens my credibility up to more potshots.*

*Solution: Find alternative method of insemination.*

With a hollow ache where his heart used to be Caleb closed the book and dropped it back on the bench. She'd written the entry a week ago, but for Brooke, he was nothing but an alternative method of insemination.

Could he live with that?

Could he live without her?

He'd gone into this relationship knowing that their agreement was nothing more than a business proposition for Brooke, but he'd forgotten to keep his heart out of the deal. He was falling for her.

He had to get out of this house, out of the room that they'd shared and get his head together. He needed to pack, because he couldn't sleep in that bed knowing that to Brooke he was no more than a living donor. Make that a *specimen.*

He wanted Brooke. No doubt about it. Waking up beside her felt right. Too right. And it scared the hell out of him. He should have known it was too good to be true. An optimistic woman who lived for the future didn't belong with a bitter man who'd spent years trying to change his past.

He charged right past the corral full of horses and guests waiting for their last morning ride.

"Hey, bro. Who put a fire under your tail?" Patrick called after him.

Caleb picked up a rock and pitched it as far as he could. "Shoot me now. Put me outta my misery."

"Uh-oh. Those words are only said under the influence of tequila or a woman. Never know you to drink so early. So it must be Brooke."

He wasn't in the mood for the smart-aleck grin on his brother's face. "Go chase a skirt."

"By the way, do you know you have another hickey?"

"Shut up."

"You're usually a morning person. What happened to put you in such a foul mood? You gonna confess or do I have to go to the source?"

How could he explain that he'd agreed to deliberately get a woman pregnant? To Patrick that amounted to deliberately exposing yourself to rabies.

"Does it have anything to do with the not-so-subtle questions you asked Brand at the hospital?" His brother, as usual, was persistent.

Hell, Patrick would find out soon enough. He might as well tell him and get it over with. "Brooke's willing to give me the Double C."

Patrick laughed. "Yeah right, and what does she want for it? Your firstborn?" When Caleb didn't laugh Patrick's grin faded. "You're not going to do something stupid, are you?"

He already had. Probably the stupidest thing he'd ever done in his life. "Brooke wants a baby. I agreed to father her child in exchange for all but a hundred acres and the Double C homestead."

But could he follow through with the plan, knowing she was ashamed of him? He wanted her to be happy and she believed a baby would make her happy.

Patrick swore. "It's just dirt, Caleb."

"It's our history. Landers have owned this land for over a hundred years. I'm the reason we lost it. I'm the one who has to get it back."

"Nobody ever blamed you."

"I blame myself. I could have stopped Amanda's spending spree and I didn't."

"No, because you were trying to make amends with

her brother, but Whitt dumped you, Caleb. Friends who bail at the first sign of trouble aren't worth hanging on to.''

Patrick had a point. Could he walk away from his deal with Brooke and the Double C? Could he forget the land he'd spent ten years fighting for? Could he forget Brooke?

No, times three.

Patrick looked uncomfortable. ''Aren't you forgetting something, bro?''

''What?'' He didn't have the patience for riddles.

''You had the mumps when you were eleven.''

''And your point is?''

''That mumps can cause sterility.''

A cold knot formed in Caleb's stomach. ''That's an old wives' tale.''

''Is it? Best I can remember, Amanda said it was your fault she didn't get pregnant after the wedding.''

For one foolish year he'd tried to make the best of his marriage. Amanda had believed a kid would help, and he'd let her convince him to try. ''It's a rare side effect. Besides, it's a good thing Amanda didn't get pregnant since she ended up running off with Junior.''

''Look, I'm not trying to play devil's advocate here, but the point is, it happens. You should get it checked out.''

If he shot blanks Brooke wouldn't want him. The decision about whether or not he could live without her or his family's land would be taken out of his hands. He massaged the tense muscles in the back of his neck and studied the bright blue sky.

''The land means that much to you?''

''Patrick, I know you don't give a flip about the ranch, but ranching isn't just what I do. It's who I am. Hell, you'd probably rather run the dude ranch than ride herd.''

''Well, yeah. There's somebody to talk to besides the cows and ranch hands that smell worse than you.''

Caleb let the insult pass. He listened to the guests laughing and talking. He heard Toby call everybody together for a rundown of the final morning's activities, and then he heard somebody ask for Brooke. His insides clenched. If he was infertile, managing the Double C could be as close as he'd ever get to owning it again, and it was the only way he'd be near Brooke.

No matter what kind of mess he'd made of his personal life he had to go back and do his duty. He took one step toward the festivities, but Patrick stepped in front of him.

"I can't believe I'm saying this when I'm sober as a judge, but if all she wants is a kid…I guess I could do it—if you can't, that is."

The thought of Patrick's baby in Brooke's belly made him sick to his stomach. "No."

But Patrick wasn't listening. "I mean, I'm not ever going to get married."

"No."

"And Brooke's all right. She does dress kind of funny wearing all those Easter egg colors, but—"

"*No,* dammit." Before he knew it he had Patrick's shirt in his fists and his brother dangling off the ground.

"Hey, you're wrinkling my shirt. Turn me loose before I make you."

The haze of jealousy subsided. Caleb slowly unclenched his fingers. He wasn't thinking straight. He'd been on the verge of messing up his brother's face. He shoved and Patrick staggered back a few steps. "Quit pushing my buttons."

Patrick grinned. "You're an easy mark. She's got you, man. You're kicking like a steer at the end of a short rope."

Caleb called his brother some of the names his mother had once washed his mouth out for using.

Patrick only laughed. "So when are you supposed to do the deed?"

Caleb swallowed, but the knot in his throat refused to budge. "We're working on it."

"Didn't anybody ever tell you that regular sex is supposed to improve your attitude?"

"Then what's your problem?"

Patrick grimaced. "Ouch. How is it that you and Brand manage to find the women with screwball plans? First you married Amanda who only saw you as her ticket outta McMullen County, and now Brooke wants you to stud her. Couldn't you just find a normal gal with no ulterior motives to scratch your itch?"

He didn't itch around normal women. He preferred the ones who talked in catchy phrases, wore prissy colors and tackled a problem straight-on.

Even though he'd refused to provide a sample in a test tube for her before, it looked like he'd have to do so now to rule out sterility and to determine his value as a potential husband. He wouldn't propose if he couldn't give her the family she wanted. And list or no list, Brooke was more important than his pride.

"The guests are checking out today. I'll be moving back home. If you've put any of your junk into my room you'd better get it out."

Patrick shook his head. "You're making a mistake. If you love her you need to stay here and tell her."

Hearing the L-word out of Patrick's mouth left him almost speechless. "I never said I loved her."

"Didn't have to. You've been walking around with a sappy smile on your face since she gave you that first hickey."

Yeah, he probably had. The uptight lady had hooked him that first night when she'd unwound all over him. He'd just been too slow to know it. "Anybody ever tell you that you talk too much?"

"Only my older brother, but I don't listen to him."

Brooke sat at the head table beside the podium chewing an antacid and wondering what she'd say to eight thousand SuperMart employees when her very belief system was crumbling beneath her.

Not only were her goals external and dependent on others, but her near panic over having failed to meet them by her thirty-fifth birthday contradicted her belief that failure was part of the process of personal growth.

That fear of failure had driven her to making spontaneous choices she normally wouldn't make, choices which led her to a man who made her step outside her comfort zone on a regular basis. And she'd begun to like it.

The cylinders clicked into place and she sat up straighter. *That* was why Caleb had come into her life. He was here to make her realize that she'd taken a wrong turn and to guide her to the correct path. He questioned her and tested her when she'd stopped questioning and testing herself. She'd accused him of being in a rut when *she* was the one stuck on the wrong path.

The temptation to write down her discovery nearly overwhelmed her, but she resisted the urge to dig out a pen and write on the back of the evening's program. Caleb was right. Her Day Planner *was* a crutch and she'd deliberately left it behind. It kept her from facing reality. It kept her from thinking outside the box. *Habits,* she'd written in her third book, *blocked the potential for original thinking.*

She'd written of respecting those around you, and yet she hadn't respected Caleb's goals. He wasn't the underachiever she'd assumed him to be. He was a man happy in his own skin and with his own measure of success.

He was a man generous enough to show her that the faults she was trying to correct weren't faults at all.

He wasn't uncomfortable with her fame. He didn't try to ride her coattails or leech off her.

Brooke readily admitted that she had a life most would envy. She made enough money to do as she pleased. She could travel or not, depending on her desire. She didn't want her siblings' lives. She *liked* her life, so what did it matter if her mother didn't? And why had it taken Caleb to point it out?

The baby was a different matter altogether. She loved children. Some of her greatest sessions had been with learning disabled kids. They needed to know that they could go as high as they dreamed despite their special challenges, as long as they were willing to work hard and seek out alternative strategies. When she left one of those sessions she could see a fire in the children's eyes that hadn't been there before and she knew she put it there. Her success in reaching those kids made her feel good about herself.

She couldn't wait to get home and tell Caleb what she'd discovered. It startled her that when she thought of home she thought not of the perfectly decorated apartment she'd given up in San Francisco, but of the Double C with its oversize furniture and expansive land. Mostly she thought of the dark-haired, slow-talking cowboy with a crooked grin and a kind heart.

She touched her belly and wondered if his child already grew within her. She'd be thrilled if it did, but if it didn't, she and Caleb could spend some time getting to know each other before they started a family.

The CEO finished his speech and called her name. Adrenaline shot through her and she sprang to her feet. Suddenly she knew exactly what she'd talk about tonight: detours, mistakes and stepping outside the comfort zone on a regular basis. Most important, she'd talk about listening to your intuition and following wherever it might lead. There was nothing wrong with planning ahead, but you had to be smart enough to recognize a better opportunity when it appeared.

Caleb would call it trusting your gut. She called it following your heart. And that was exactly what she intended to do from now on.

She stepped behind the podium and smiled at the sea of faces. "Detours happen. A winner will find a way back to the right road...."

# Twelve

The dude ranch was quiet when Brooke pulled into the driveway. Rico met her at the car and she took a moment to pet him. She practically skipped up the sidewalk. She shoved open the front door and smiled when she realized she'd been humming "Happy Trails."

"Caleb?" Her voice echoed back. "Maria?"

"Caleb's not here," Maria called from the kitchen.

"Did he say what time he'd be back?"

"Tomorrow morning before the dudes get here. He moved back to Crooked Creek. Said you didn't need him here anymore since none of the next batch of dudes will be staying in the main house." Maria picked up a familiar Day Planner from the credenza. "He said to give you this as soon as you got home."

A prickle of unease skipped down Brooke's spine but she dismissed it. Caleb wouldn't read her personal papers.

Would he? She thought of the lists she'd made, of how they'd hurt him if he read them. He wouldn't understand how blind and misguided she'd been when she wrote them.

"I've only been to Caleb's on horseback. Can you give me directions by car?"

Caleb paced the kitchen. He didn't dare leave the house and miss the doctor's call. He was so touchy about the humiliating appointment at the fertility clinic that his father and brother had packed a lunch and left rather than eat here.

A car door slammed out front. Before he could head for the door, the phone rang. His stomach knotted. Bracing himself, he reached for the receiver. When he heard the telemarketer's spiel he exhaled and turned toward the front door. Brooke stood on the other side of the screen, wearing the lavender suit she'd been wearing the night they met. He hung up the phone in the middle of a sales pitch.

She opened the door and stepped inside. "Hi."

God, he loved her smile. Would today be the last time he'd see it? He couldn't find his voice so he jerked a nod.

"Miami was great, but I am so glad to be home."

"Brooke—"

She walked purposefully toward him. The frisky glint in her eye told him she wanted to play. "What was it you said about a kitchen table?"

His blood pressure—among other things—rose.

"Where's your family?"

"Other side of the ranch, but—"

"Good." She reached for the knot at her waist and tugged the belt free. "Do I have to tie you up or are you going to cooperate?"

His red blood cells herded and headed south. He should stop her and explain about the doctor's visit, but he didn't. This might be the last time he'd get to touch her, to taste her, to hear her make that sexy noise. "You already have me tied up."

She smiled and unfastened her skirt. It slithered to the

floor and she stepped out of it. Her jacket fluttered after it. She stood before him in her heels and the tiniest bra and panties he'd ever seen. "Like these? I bought them for you."

She pivoted slowly and he nearly swallowed his tongue. He only had a second to admire her sweetly curved, *bare* behind in the thong before the bra and briefs hit the floor. He could barely breathe. His legs felt weak and he had to lean against the table for support.

"*You* are overdressed." She ripped open his shirt snaps and reached for his belt buckle. Smiling up at him, she winked. "The first time is going to be fast. I'll make it up to you later."

She quoted his words from their first night back at him and fell to her knees to drive him slam out of his mind.

He let her for about ten seconds, and then he scooped his hands under her arms and tugged her upward.

A frown puckered her brow. "You don't like—"

He cut her off with a kiss. Depending on the results of this morning's test, he might never get to tell her he loved her, but he could show her. He put every drop of emotion he had into his kiss and his touch.

He wanted to go slow, to savor every second, but Brooke wouldn't let him. Her greedy hands were everywhere, igniting fires and hurrying him along. She tore her mouth away to bite and lick his chin, his neck, his chest, his…

He sucked in a sharp breath and pulled her back up again. He tried to map each inch of her exposed skin, storing away the memories…just in case. When he couldn't wait any longer he lifted her onto the table and thrust deep inside her. She was hot and slick and so wet he groaned aloud.

Brooke wrapped her legs around his waist and dug her nails into his buttocks. Her whispered pleas urged him on. Greedily he sampled her neck and her breasts with his hands and his mouth. He speared his fingers through her hair and angled her head so that he could taste her cries of pleasure on his tongue.

When she arched off the table and jerked in his arms, he emptied himself as close to her womb as he could get.

His legs trembled. His heart raced. He braced his arms on either side of her and memorized her sexy, satisfied smile. Once he told her his news, it might vanish forever.

He smoothed a hand over her mussed hair. "You know there's a perfectly good bed upstairs."

"Really? Why don't you show me?"

Curling his hands beneath her bottom, he lifted her. "Hold on."

Slowly—due to his pants being almost around his knees—he carried her up the stairs to his room and laid her on the bed. She scooted under the covers and beckoned for him. When he saw the happiness in her eyes, he knew he couldn't keep his secret and risk disappointing her later.

"Brooke—"

The serious expression on Caleb's face made her uneasy. Whatever he was going to say, she knew she didn't want to hear it. She snuggled close and kissed him, putting every ounce of the passion he'd unleashed into it. When the stiffness left his limbs, she drew back a fraction.

"You were right to question me during my workshop. Your questions led to a revelation in Miami. I've been trying to please the wrong people. My mother, my publisher, the public. I was competing with my brother and sister even though as you pointed out, I didn't want their lives. I love mine."

The wariness remained on his face. She scooted closer and hooked her thigh over his. Caleb desired her. She feared that might be the only emotion he felt.

*The journey to your heart's desire begins with the first step.* Second book, opening line.

"I got off track, and you pulled me back, Caleb. You jolted me out of the rut I'd been traveling in. You made me look at my life from a different perspective, and you showed me that I was taking life far too seriously. You made me have fun when I'd cut all fun out of my life.''

Tension knotted in her stomach when he opened his mouth to speak. She rushed on, hoping to delay whatever bad news he might deliver. ''My rival condemned me and he was right to do so because I was miserable and stressing out. I lived off antacids for the simple reason that I wasn't practicing my own principles.''

''I wondered how long it would take you to figure that out.''

She smiled. ''I wouldn't have without you.''

''Brooke...''

''Caleb—'' Whatever was causing the sadness in his eyes, she knew she didn't want to hear it.

He put a finger over her mouth. ''I might not be able to get you pregnant.''

Her smile faded and her heart sank. ''I don't understand.''

''I had mumps as a kid. There's a chance I may be...sterile.''

She took a few slow breaths. Her heart pounded against her ribs, and then acceptance settled over her. She wanted to have Caleb's children, but she didn't need to be a mother to make her life complete.

She cupped his cheek and met his gaze. ''It's okay, Caleb, because the second most important thing I realized in Miami was that I wanted a child for the wrong reasons. I get great feedback when I work with kids. I can look in their eyes and see that I've made a difference, but I can do that without actually giving birth to them.''

His brow pleated. ''It's not the same.''

''There are other ways for us to have a family.''

''A family?''

''Yes, you and I and our family.''

''You're willing to risk career suicide?''

She grimaced. ''You read my journal.''

"It fell on the floor opened to my assets and liabilities."

She'd hurt him. "I was wrong when I wrote those, Caleb."

He shook his head. "I *am* uneducated."

"No, you're self-taught."

"I haven't traveled."

"We'll travel together."

"What about my lack of ambition?"

She bit her lip and wrinkled her nose. She'd been narrow-minded, foolish and blind. "That was my failure to recognize your goals, not your failure to have any. I was measuring your goals with my yardstick. You are your only competition."

"What about your parents? I don't want your mother giving you a migraine over me."

She sighed and laid her head on his chest. "My mother has a very strange way of challenging us to do better. She pits my brother, sister and I against each other like we're opponents. But we're not. We're different people with different needs."

"And your rival?"

She hated the doubts she'd put on his face. "My rival can say whatever he likes, because as long as I'm happy with the choices I've made then that's all that matters. And I am happy, Caleb, happier than I've been in a long time. Because of you." She twined his chest hair around her finger. Hesitantly she asked, "Do you want to know the most important thing I discovered?"

He jerked a nod.

"That I love you."

His chest rose with a swiftly indrawn breath. "Brooke—"

She pressed her fingers to his lips. "You don't have to say anything. I just wanted you to know. You gave me back the joy in my life, Caleb. You put me back on the right path. My love is my gift to you. And baby or no baby, I want you to have your land."

He covered her hand with his, kissed her fingertips, and then pulled her hand away. The tender look in his eyes made her heart skip a beat. "I love you, too, but a deal's a deal. We have a contract and I'll honor my part."

Brooke's eyes started to burn. She wanted to laugh and cry at the same time. She cuddled up to Caleb, loving the feel of the man who'd grounded her to the most important things in life. She'd been chasing rainbows for so long, and she'd finally found her pot of gold in a down-to-earth cowboy. "I wish we could stay here forever."

"I'll lay in a supply of food and lock the door."

Brooke laughed. His dry humor was just one of the things she loved about him. "Not only do we have guests arriving tomorrow morning, I have to fly to Las Vegas next weekend."

His chest heaved beneath her cheek. "Vegas?"

"I have a speaking engagement."

His fingers feathered through her hair. "I'll come with you."

She knew the decision didn't come from a need to share her spotlight. Why would he want to leave his beloved ranch and come along? "What about the dude ranch?"

"Let Patrick handle it for a while. He took his turn helping Charlie. He knows how."

"Okay."

Caleb shifted so that they lay facing each other. Concentration tightened his features and darkened his eyes. "Brooke, we both know how you are about long-term relationships. Could we just skip that part and get straight to the I do's?"

Her breath caught and she jerked upright. "Are you proposing?"

Wincing, Caleb sat up beside her. "Yeah, and I'm not doing it right. I don't have a ring and I'm not on my knees—"

She caught his arm as he tried to roll off the bed. "I've done it that way. Let's do it differently this time." She pulled him back down beside her and tangled her legs with his. "So, you were saying?"

"I was saying that I love your little ditties and your catalog cowgirl clothes. I love the way you tackle any challenge, and the way you refuse to let me live in the past. I love the way you took in the ugliest dog on the planet because he needed a friend. But mostly…I love you, Brooke Blake."

A tear slid down her cheek and she leaned forward to whisper against his lips, "Not as much as I love you, cowboy."

The phone rang. Caleb tensed up all over. Brooke had agreed to marry him. She didn't think his infertility would be a problem, but he wasn't so sure he liked being damaged goods. She deserved better. He took a deep breath and reached for the receiver.

Brooke, with a mischievous sparkle in her eyes, slid beneath the covers. Her tongue dipped into his navel and he nearly dropped the phone.

"Lander," he choked out his name when she moved lower.

"Mr. Lander, this is Susie at the Dodson Clinic. We have the results from your test. I've called to tell you that everything is normal. Did you have any questions?"

Relief washed over him. "No, ma'am. Thanks." He hung up.

His breath caught when Brooke's fingers curled around him and he choked out a laugh. "Hey, lady, that's a loaded weapon in your hands. Be careful how you use it."

Brooke poked her head out of the covers. A curious smile curved her lips.

Caleb couldn't keep the grin off his face. "That was the doctor's office. I took a little visit into town today, and I don't think we'll have trouble with that family you wanted after all."

# Epilogue

Caleb grinned at himself in the mirrored ceiling of the big round bed in the honeymoon suite of the Las Vegas hotel. He and Brooke had tied the knot last night right after she'd finished her program. Two hours of listening to her little ditties had turned him on so much he hadn't been able to wait another day to marry her. He'd dragged her to the nearest wedding chapel which didn't have an Elvis impersonator.

On the way back to the hotel Brooke had come out of her shell with a vengeance. She'd ducked into an all-night lingerie store to buy him a surprise wedding gift which they'd never gotten around to opening last night. A few minutes ago she'd ducked into the bathroom with that gift still concealed in a bag. The wicked promise in her eyes had his blood fizzing in anticipation of unwrapping it—and her—very slowly. His grin broadened.

Her scream doused his mounting excitement. He vaulted from bed, raced across the room and skidded to a stop in the doorway. Brooke stood in the middle of the bathroom floor. She wasn't cut or bleeding and she looked…fabulous…incredible…hotter than sin in an X-rated cowgirl outfit. Sheer lace. Bare skin.

His blood pressure soared. For the life of him he couldn't figure out why she'd screamed. He blinked, trying to clear the sexual haze and reassessed her.

Her color fluctuated between pink and pale. Her eyes were wide and the hand holding a little white stick trembled. "Oh. My. God. I'm pregnant."

Elation filled him with warmth and excitement. He pumped his fist in the air. *"Yes."*

He stepped forward to sweep her into his arms but a sobering thought jerked him to a stop. Cupping her shoulders, he held her at arm's length. "This doesn't mean we have to stop trying, does it?"

She donned the serious expression that told him another little ditty was on the way. He couldn't stifle his grin.

"Remaining successful means continually honing your skills."

He waggled his brows and slid his fingertips beneath the lacy garter-gun belt which held up her black fishnet stockings. "I love it when you talk like a self-help manual, and I love this outfit."

He scooped her up, carried her to the rumpled bed and gently laid her in the center. He pressed a hand to her flat belly. The next generation of Landers lay beneath his fingertips. He and Brooke were going to have a family and a future together on Crooked Creek.

His chest tightened and his eyes stung. When he'd plotted to get his land back he'd never envisioned sharing it with anyone but his brothers. Now he couldn't picture the place without his catalog cowgirl and her catchy phrases. And their kids. An armadillo-size knot clogged his throat.

She smoothed his hair and cupped the back of his neck. "You were great last night."

He leered and she playfully smacked his arm.

"I meant, thanks for stepping in and introducing me when the PR man couldn't make it."

He tried to shrug, but the pattern she traced across his chest had all his muscles—among other things—tensing up. "It's no big deal."

"It is. You supported my career, Caleb, and you supported me. Your pitch about the motivational workshops at the dude ranch brought a flurry of interest, and those new brochures you had printed were a wonderful surprise. We'll be booked up for a long time."

"Glad I could help."

"You did. Thank you." She worried her lower lip with her teeth. "And now I need your help with something else. In the past year I've learned everything possible about getting pregnant and staying that way, but I know absolutely nothing about being a mother."

"Not a problem. I'm sure Brand and Toni will let us baby-sit the twins. You'll get all the practice you need. Besides, if the way you baby that dog is anything to go by, you'll do fine."

"You're an incredibly generous man, Caleb Lander. You're always thinking of someone else, but all Rico needed was someone to love him."

"A baby needs the same thing. In the meantime, remember positive thoughts yield positive outcomes."

Her brows rose. "Why, Caleb, I believe that was a little ditty." She arched up and feathered a kiss across his lips, his chin, his neck.

He chuckled. "Do they turn you on as much as they do me?"

She glanced at him from beneath her lashes, and he knew he was in for the sweetest torture of his life.

Brooke's laugh was sexy and full of her newfound confidence in herself as a woman. The mischief in her eyes promised trouble, and he did *love* her brand of trouble.

* * * * *

# COMING NEXT MONTH

**#1513 SHAMELESS—Ann Major**
*Lone Star Country Club*
With danger nipping at her heels, Celeste Cavanaugh turned to rancher Phillip Westin, her very capable, very *good-looking* ex. Though Phillip still drove her crazy with his take-charge ways, it wasn't long before he and Celeste were back in each other's arms. But this time Celeste was playing for keeps…and she was shamelessly in love!

**#1514 BEAUTY & THE BLUE ANGEL—Maureen Child**
*Dynasties: The Barones*
When soon-to-be-single-mom Daisy Cusack went into labor on the job, help came in the form of sexy navy pilot Alex Barone. Before she knew it, Daisy was in danger of falling for her handsome white knight. Alex was everything she'd dreamed of, but what would happen when his leave ended?

**#1515 PRINCESS IN HIS BED—Leanne Banks**
*The Royal Dumonts*
The minute he saw the raven-haired beauty who'd crashed into his barn, rancher Jared McNeil knew he was in trouble. Then Mimi Deerman agreed to work off her debt by caring for his nieces. Jared sensed Mimi had secrets, but playing house with her had undeniable benefits, and Jared soon longed to make their temporary arrangement permanent. Little did he know that his elegant nanny was really a princess in disguise!

**#1516 THE GENTRYS: ABBY—Linda Conrad**
*The Gentrys*
Though Comanche Gray Wolf Parker had vowed not to get involved with a woman not chosen by his tribal elders, after green-eyed Abby Gentry saved his life, he was honor-bound to help her. When Abby's brother tried to arrange a marriage for her, Gray suggested a pretend engagement. But the heat they generated was all too real, and Gray was torn between love and duty.

**#1517 MAROONED WITH A MILLIONAIRE—Kristi Gold**
*The Baby Bank*
The last thing millionaire recluse Jackson Dunlap wanted was the company of spunky, pregnant Lizzie Matheson. But after he rescued the fun-loving blond enchantress from a hot-air balloon and they wound up stranded on his boat, he found himself utterly defenseless against her many charms. If he didn't know better, he'd say he was falling in love!

**#1518 SLEEPING WITH THE PLAYBOY—Julianne MacLean**
Sleeping with her client was *not* part of bodyguard Jocelyn MacKenzie's job description, but Donovan Knight was pure temptation. The charismatic millionaire made her feel feminine *and* powerful, but if they were to have a future together, Jocelyn would have to confront her fears and insecurities…and finally lay them to rest.